Book One, Awaken

Fated Saga Fantasy Series

Rachel Humphrey - D'aigle

AWAKEN

Chapter 1

Colin Jacoby did not hear the morning birds chirping.

He did not feel the black fly tickling his arm, or the cool morning breeze blowing through his wavy, bowl-cut hair.

More importantly, however, is what he did *not* hear approaching.

A fallen tree branch, just a few feet away, snapped under stalking footsteps.

Colin's head jerked up. His book slipped from his hands, falling onto the muddy ground, as the color drained from his face.

There was no escape.

Toady number one blocked him from the right, while toady number two blocked the left, leaving the head bully blocking the pathway in front.

A sheer granite rock towered behind Colin.

"Hi –hi guys," he stammered, putting on a fake smile. "I see you're all camping here again this summer, too."

"Lucky us," snarled the head bully bitterly. "Only thing good about it, is gettin' to pound on little kids like *you*."

Colin could not decide if he should be more upset over the impending humiliation, or at being called a little kid.

"If you recall," he began, hoping to distract them, "I believe I am actually older than the three of you." He laughed nervously after he had said it.

The head bully was easily a foot taller and wider than Colin. The bullies face boiled with rage as he furiously strode toward Colin, pushing him to the muddy ground.

His two toadies pointed and shrieked with laughter.

Colin, defeated, prepared for whatever was to come next: a mouthful of mud, a wedgie, or maybe this time, a black eye.

Then he saw it!

The thing Colin Jacoby dreaded the most.

The silhouette of a girl dressed in black.

"Not her too!" he uttered, letting his face fall into the mud.

The girl's voice rang out tauntingly.

"I thought I made it clear that only *I* get to bully my little brother?" She stood atop a nearby tree stump, her flame-red hair blowing in the breeze.

The head bully jumped back, startled, dropping his smug grin.

"Meghan Jacoby. H-hey. We weren't doin' notin'." He backed up a few steps adding, "He fell on his own!" The bully scurried off, his two toadies at his heels.

Meghan jumped off her perch with a satisfied smirk.

"I should have just given him two more black eyes," she boasted. She held out her hand, offering to help her brother off the ground. "You can thank me any time, Little Bro."

Colin stubbornly ignored the offer and dragged himself out of the mud. He collected his mud-ruined book and walked toward home. Meghan's longer stride easily allowed her to catch up and she sauntered alongside him.

"Okay. Fine. Don't thank me."

Colin still did not answer.

"Nice move by the way," she continued, ignoring his brooding demeanor. Mockingly she repeated, "*I think I am actually older than you...* good way to get your head bit off, Little Bro."

Colin stopped abruptly, clenching his teeth. "I tried to block you."

"Yeah, I sensed that. Why?"

"Maybe I am tired of having someone in my head all the time!"

"You think you're tired of it! Your head is exhausting."

"Then why don't you stay out?"

3

"So you would rather have your face full of mud and your underwear pulled up over your head right now, then?"

Colin, now fuming, stormed away as fast as his short legs would allow him.

Could there be anything worse than his sister coming to his rescue? The fact that she was his *younger* sister (yes, by only two minutes, but still younger), would always make it worse!

"Ah! Will I ever grow?" he screamed silently, successfully blocking the thought from her.

As they neared the campsite, Meghan, sensing his irritation, attempted to smooth things over.

"Colin, we can't help that we hear each other's thoughts. Just try a little harder to block me out if you don't want me to hear." It did not have the helpful effect that she hoped it would.

Colin stepped around her and into their uncle's travel trailer. Their uncle, Arnon Jacoby, sat inside, tinkering on a toaster. His eyes widened at the sight of Colin, covered in mud, but before he could ask what had happened, Colin spat out, "Don't ask!" and disappeared into the bathroom.

"Don't tell me those same bullies are back again?" Arnon asked Meghan, when she entered a moment later. She nodded yes and sat down, helping herself to a glass of juice.

"I wonder if I should have a talk with their parents."

"Yeah! If you wanna get him killed!" she scolded her uncle.

"You're probably right," he agreed after a moment.

"Oh, almost forgot," said Meghan, as she uncovered a slow cooker and stirred the contents inside. "I ran into Kanda on my way to find Colin. She's coming for breakfast."

Meghan dropped the spoon into the slow cooker as a loud buzzer went off, startling her.

"I thought for sure I had fixed that," exclaimed Arnon.

Meghan raced into the hallway opening the door to the dryer, instantly returning quiet to the trailer.

"Well, it's at least drying now," she yelled, grabbing the clothes. She threw the laundry on the kitchen table and deftly folded each item, except for her own. She put away her uncle's and her brother's, but when it came to her own she simply threw them on the floor, on top of another pile from a previous load.

Colin, fresh from showering, appeared in their shared room. He ignored Meghan, sulking his way to his dresser.

Each twin had a tall bunk bed with a desk, chair and dresser underneath. At the foot of each bed, shoved into a small shelf, was a TV and DVD player. Colin had added another shelf, along side the trailer's wall, for his many books.

Colin unhooked a curtain, which dropped and divided the room, allowing him privacy while dressing. A few minutes later, he pulled the curtain back, hooking it to the wall and started up his laptop. While waiting, he plugged in his ear buds. Before he could hit play on his I-pod, his sister inhaled in a deep gasp, holding her breath.

"What?" he asked, annoyed and not yet in the mood to speak to her. He heard the thought before she could say it. "Did you lose the locket?" he prompted. His mood changed immediately to concern.

Meghan felt through her sweater, exhaling in relief.

"Still there," she breathed out. Meghan always wore the locket, for safekeeping. However, neither twin would have wanted to lose it, as it had once belonged to their mother. The locket was the only possession of hers that they still owned.

Two vines, one colored black and the other gold, covered the outside of the locket, twisting around each other like a snake. The most confusing part, though, was that the vines had actual sharp, piercing thorns, which if Meghan bent or moved just right would pinch her skin. Over time, the occasional prick of the thorns had become a comfort to her, a positive affirmation that it was still securely hanging around her neck.

Colin turned his attention back to his laptop and I-pod, but again, found his thoughts interrupted. "What now?" he grumbled.

"Can't find my black jacket. Need to sew a button back on."

"How can you find anything? It's all in a pile, and everything in that pile is black. Even the carpet it's piled on is black." He turned on his I-pod, trying to block out the moans of disgust seeping into his own thoughts. After a few minutes of tearing through her side of the room, she gave up, leaving.

A moment later, she yelled that breakfast was ready. As Colin entered the kitchen, Meghan gently pulled the ear buds out of his ears and ordered him to set the outside table.

"Why are there four plates on the counter?" he asked, instantly suspect.

Meghan smiled, blocking her thoughts, but it took him only a second to guess.

"Kanda's coming. Yes!"

Meghan knew how much Colin loved Kanda Macawi, especially the stories she told around the campfire. Meghan knew this would also brighten Colin's mood.

Uncle Arnon grabbed the coffee and juice, while Meghan brought two slow cookers full of food out to the table. An enclosed screened room protected them from the thousands of newly born mosquitoes whose only purpose was to find their next blood-filled meal.

Footsteps approached the Jacoby campsite. Meghan, Colin and Arnon watched eagerly as an attractive Native American woman strode closer. She wore a thin, full-length sweater to stave off the chilly morning air. When she arrived, Uncle Arnon held open the screen door, allowing her entrance to the mosquito-free zone; he zipped it up hastily after she stepped inside.

"My dearest friends," she said. "Back at my campground again." After hugs all around, she demanded, "What have you done with the real Meghan Jacoby? Look at you! On the corner of thirteen and growing like a vine." She gazed closely at Meghan's face, zoning in on an ocean blue gem in her nose.

"Awesome, isn't it? Uncle Arnon got it for me as an early birthday present."

"I thought," started Kanda, in an I-told-you-so tone, "you were going to make her wait another year?"

"You know Meghan," replied Arnon. "She can be very... persuasive."

Meghan curtsied knowingly.

"You will visit me later, Meghan," ordered Kanda, as Meghan rounded the table, serving breakfast. "I've got something that will help the infection."

Meghan unconsciously touched the blue gem. It did hurt a little. How did Kanda always know?

"I have to agree on the *awesome* part," Kanda continued. "It matches perfectly with your eyes." She winked mischievously and swept her attention to Colin. The boy whom would also be turning thirteen soon, but, who had not grown a single inch during the last year.

"My, what a good looking young man you are turning into. Is it possible that you look even smarter than you did last summer?" She worded her compliment carefully.

Colin's face lit up. Kanda always knew how to make him feel better. She then took hold of Arnon's hand.

"I'm sorry I was not here when you arrived last night. I had some business that just could not wait. I am just so happy that you're back, Arnon."

His cheeks blushed slightly as he showed Kanda to her seat.

Meghan's breakfast, was as usual, scrumptious. She had one slow cooker filled with pumpkin oatmeal, and the other with cinnamon bread pudding.

In no time, their bellies were full and content.

As they finished, a host of muffled footsteps filtered in from the entrance of Cobbscott Campground.

"What is that?" muttered Uncle Arnon.

A moment later, a large group of people came trudging along the camp road.

"Gypsies," determined their uncle. The color drained from his face as he said it.

Kanda jumped up to greet the new arrivals. "I've been expecting them. I must go, but I'll be back, Arnon."

Arnon did not hear her. He stepped back towards the trailer, watching from the shadows as the procession marched by.

The Gypsies were not what the twins expected. Other than the fact that they each carried trunks, packages or suitcases stuffed with belongings, they did not look like other Gypsies the twins had encountered during previous travels.

The men wore polished winged-tipped shoes with brightly colored shirts, and many of the women dressed in thin, shapely, long jackets. One man in particular stood out, with his colorfully spiked hair, black tattoos that slithered out of his hairline, and by the fact that he wore a boisterous, full-length winter coat in early summer.

One of the younger Gypsies, a tall and scrawny boy, glanced in the twins' direction. His stringy hair hid most of his face, but his eyes made contact with Colin and then Meghan. Just as quickly as he'd made the contact, he severed it.

The Gypsies greeted Kanda and she walked with them, showing them to their campsites.

"It makes sense now," said Meghan, unexpectedly.

"What makes sense now?" asked Arnon.

"Why those Gypsy wagons are always parked in the campground. They must leave them here, to use when they return."

Arnon nodded in agreement and then lost his balance, falling back onto the trailer steps. Even in the dark shadow of the trailer, the twins could see his face turn from white to green.

"You all right, Uncle Arnon?" asked Meghan. *He looks like he is going to be sick* she thought.

Or, like he has seen a ghost added Colin, in his own mind.

"Yes, yes I'm fine," Arnon finally answered after a tense minute of silence. "You two go clean up breakfast. I'm going to wait for Kanda to come back," he said in a manner that indicated it would be a private conversation.

The twins did not argue. They each gathered dishes and leftover food, heading into the trailer. Once inside, Meghan washed the dishes, while Colin dried. Half way through, and in unison, the twins shuddered, as an eerie tingle crawled down their spines. It brought them out of their silent stupor over their uncle's unusual behavior.

"Was that your creepy feeling or mine?" asked Colin.

"We felt it at the same time," said Meghan. "Bad omen if you ask me."

Colin hated when Meghan said things like that. They had an eerie way of coming true.

They tried to shake off the eerie feeling and finish with the clean up, all the while keeping an eye on their uncle, who still sat on the step, appearing now to be in deep concentration. They heard Kanda's voice call out to him and he walked methodically, meeting her in the middle of the now empty roadway.

The twins were curious about their uncle's strange reaction to the Gypsies and strained their ears to hear the conversation, but heard nothing but unintelligible echoes.

"I did not wish to worry you, Arnon," began Kanda. "I was afraid if I told you *this* was the summer... oh, honestly, Arnon, I was half afraid you would take the twins and disappear."

Instinct did tell him to grab his two young traveling companions and run far away, but he fought that instinct realizing he could not act upon it.

"You know me too well, Kanda." His eyes wandered toward the Gypsies campsites. "My betrayal to *them* I can handle. But my impending betrayal to my young companions..." he left the sentence unfinished, knowing Kanda already understood his anguish.

She took hold of Arnon's hand and squeezed it firmly, forcing him to realize the truth.

I do not need to run anymore. This thought brought him relief, followed instantly by regret for feeling that relief. *This is the moment I have feared more than any other in my life. All our lives will change now. Is this good or bad? Are they ready? Do they have a choice?* All of Arnon's fears came pouring out at once, forcing him to take a deep, cleansing breath to regain his composure.

"Maybe we…" he stopped, closing his eyes. He did not dare speak his wishes aloud.

Kanda dropped his hand gently.

"Their path lies before them, Arnon. We cannot interfere with their destiny any longer," she affirmed. "There is still a little time," she told him, in hopes of comforting his fear, if only temporarily.

He nodded, trying to ignore his growing irrepressible desire to seize the twins and run. To hide them far away from the dangers they now faced.

The twins, finished with the cleaning, exited the trailer. They saw Kanda dropping their uncle's hand.

"Do you think they like each other, Col?"

"Sure they like each other. Why would we come back every summer if they didn't?"

"I mean like-like," Meghan rephrased. "You know. Are they in *love?*"

"Oh. That. Well, if they were, don't you think Uncle Arnon would have stopped traveling around and stayed here with Kanda?"

"I can imagine a lot of things, Col. But Uncle Arnon settling down in one place is not one of them."

Kanda interrupted their conversation.

"You must all come tonight, to my fire pit," she bid them, so all could hear. "I have a grand feast prepared to welcome the summer."

Uncle Arnon forced his fears aside.

"We will be there, Kanda," he replied firmly, now back near the trailer's entrance. "Besides, I know Colin is eager to hear more of your campfire stories."

Colin's excitement showed as he beamed widely in agreement.

"And I have a special one planned for tonight," Kanda added, in a tone that sent Colin's mind reeling with curiosity, and once again reignited Arnon's fears for the twins' safety.

Kanda's mischievous eyes sparkled as her attention turned to the campground's entrance. "And now, I think more good news."

The low rumbling of the approaching motorhome was unmistakable. Meghan's heart skipped a beat. A second later Colin had guessed, too.

"The Jendayas are here!" He ran a few steps closer, waving vigorously. Meghan ducked behind the mirror on their uncle's station wagon, rechecking her clothes and hair. She wished there was time to apply a darker shade of eyeliner.

Arnon rejoined Kanda and held out his hand, inviting her to lead the way. She snatched him instead, and they walked arm and arm.

The thirty-four foot motorhome came to a slow, skidding stop. The windows rolled down and the entry door flew open. An athletic looking tall and tan boy, with crazily curly, dusty blond hair, leapt out, grinning widely.

"Sebastien, hey," said Colin.

"Hey, backatcha," the athletic boy replied, patting Colin's shoulder. Sebastien turned to hug Meghan, but she kept her distance. He blushed slightly, but did not step any closer. He opened his mouth to speak, but was interrupted by his mother.

"Don't run off, Sebastien," she said, in a controlled, but quiet manner. "You need to help your father."

"I know, Mom," he answered begrudgingly.

He and the twins walked a short distance away so they could have their own private conversation.

"I was beginning to think summer would never get here," Sebastien said.

"It was a long year this time, wasn't it?" agreed Colin. He continued without waiting for a reply. "There's a caravan of Gypsies in the campground. Did you see any of them on your drive in?"

"Gypsies? No, I haven't seen them. Where are they camped?"

"The next few sites over. You know, the ones with the permanently parked wagons," answered Meghan.

"So they are the owners of those," replied Sebastien. "Have you met any of them?"

"No," answered Colin. "And I do not intend to!"

"Oh, Little Bro, endlessly afraid," teased Meghan.

Colin frowned.

"Not afraid," he clarified. "Um, well, maybe a little afraid of *you* getting us into trouble again. And I am not getting grounded this summer!"

Meghan punched him in the arm.

Colin winced.

"I can see the two of you have not changed a bit," laughed their friend. Meghan forgot her tirade on Colin as blood rushed to her already flushed face, turning her cheeks even rosier.

A voice carried over to the trio.

"Sebastien, honey, it's time to go," called his mother.

"Let's meet up in two hours, at the secret path," he suggested, jumping back on board the motorhome. Meghan and Colin nodded their agreement. Sebastien gave them the thumbs up, which meant one thing: summer had officially started!

Two hours had not seemed like a long time to wait, but after mere minutes, the twins were already bored. Meghan kept busy by turning her room upside down in attempts to locate her lost black jacket. After finally locating it, she set up her sewing kit, outside near Colin, and sewed on a new button. Colin attempted to read a book, but let his thoughts meander every few lines or so.

"Why do you keep trying to read that book?" asked Meghan, her eyes still on her sewing project.

"Huh?" Colin had only half heard her.

"You've started it like ten times and haven't even finished the first chapter," Meghan said. "It obviously isn't any good." She cut her thread and put the needle back in her sewing kit.

Colin put the book down.

"I guess I keep trying because it is the only book I own that I have not finished. I've read everything else I own at least five times over."

"I will never understand your need to read books," Meghan replied, shaking her head. Colin could think of a hundred different, and as equally amusing, replies, but decided it was not worth the energy to get in another argument with her.

Meghan arose to put away her sewing kit, when a rustling in the bushes between their camp and the Gypsies', stopped her in her tracks. Colin slid his chair back a few feet, not thrilled at the prospect of something in the woods he could not see.

"Oh, don't be such a chicken, Col. It's too high off the ground to be anything big!" Meghan thought she saw the shadow of something in the rustling bushes and stepped a little closer. She sensed her brother's opinion that getting closer might not be the smartest idea.

"I see… something," she said softly, narrowing her eyes together, trying to focus into the bush. "Looks like a…" she fell backwards, yelping, as a bird flew out of the shrub, nearly missing a straight on collision with her face.

Colin tried to get a close look at the bird, his curiosity getting the better of him, even over the humor of his sister's shocked face. As it flew away, he could see a spiky blue-gray crest, a long, black, sharp looking bill and a white underbelly. Colin tried to recall such a bird from his books and wondered what it was.

"I saw it in there," insisted Meghan, regaining her composure. "I just couldn't get out of the way in time." She haughtily swiped dirt and pine needles off her skirt, gathered up her sewing supplies and pretended she was not the least bit surprised by what had happened.

"Sis, did you see any colors other than blue or gray?"

Meghan turned from irritated to furious at once.

"Are you serious? I almost got my face torn off by a bird and you're asking me if I got a look at its colors?" She abruptly stormed off, disappearing inside the travel trailer.

"It didn't even touch your face, you don't have to..." he stopped and blocked her mind from hearing him. "Ah, why bother? She won't listen anyway."

Colin grabbed his book and followed his sister inside. Nearly thirty minutes later she emerged from the bathroom, throwing her dirt covered skirt into the washer.

"Oh, wearing black again," teased Colin, catching the slightest wink in his uncle's eye.

"I'll dress the way I want to," she retorted.

Colin followed her into their shared room.

"I was kidding, Meghan. But even you have to admit that your clothes look a lot alike. And yet it takes you forever to get dressed."

"And that shows how much *you* know!" she snapped back. "My outfits are NEVER the same. That is *why* it takes so long. For example, and like you would notice, but I have not worn my tall black boots in days," she argued. "And I just found this sweater yesterday. I lost it weeks ago."

"Well if it all looks the same to me, I'd wager it looks the same to everyone else, too!" He knew that would infuriate her. "Besides," he continued, "I can be ready in ten minutes, tops!"

"That's pretty obvious," she snorted. "Talk about wearing the same thing every day. Khaki's, loafers, and that ridiculous vest!"

"Ridiculous? What?"

His sister plugged her nose, pretending an unbearable stench had entered the room.

"I do not stink," he sputtered, his face turning red with anger.

"That's enough!" broke in a stern voice. "You two need to stop arguing and learn to get along," scolded their uncle.

They stopped arguing, but a moment later, silently, Meghan shot a jeering thought to her brother.

"Another one for Meghan. Uh, huh. I rock!"

"I'm leaving," called out their uncle then. "Got a small job to do. Shouldn't take long." He pulled his camp hat low over his face. "Please try not to spend the rest of the day arguing," he pleaded as he stepped out of the trailer.

Arnon Jacoby was a fixer upper. He worked from camp to camp lining up jobs as they traveled. He had taken in Meghan and Colin after an accident claimed the lives of their parents, at the age of two. Having always lived on the road, he made the decision to buy a larger trailer and take them along on his travels. They had never questioned why their uncle chose this lifestyle, especially since it meant they did not have to attend normal school. Although, from the stories Sebastien had told them, they guessed that Uncle Arnon was right up there with being one of the strictest teachers ever!

Meghan closed the door to their shared room, which hid a mirror, and put on her jacket with the new button. *Another perfect fix!* She caught a side view of Colin's face and sighed, jealously.

"I wish I had your eyelashes. Any girl would die to have those, you know."

"Great!" he muttered.

"It's the truth, Col."

"I realize you are trying to be nice, Sis, but really, anything *I* have, that a girl would *die* to have, can't be a good thing."

She shook her head in disagreement.

"It's not a bad thing, Col, believe me. Girls would kill for those thick lashes of yours." She took off the jacket tossing it back to the pile-of-black on the floor. "Well there. Chores are done. You wanna go spy on our new neighbors?"

"Do I have a choice?" he returned.

"You can't hide it from me that you're curious about the Gypsies," she said.

Colin sighed.

She was right.

Again.

"Let's not take all day about it. Remember Sebastien? We are supposed to meet him soon."

"Don't worry, it won't take long," she insisted, stepping out of the trailer.

"How many emails did you get from Sebastien over the last few months, anyway?" Colin asked daringly as he followed her. She did not answer him about the emails, but her cheeks now matched the color of her flame red hair.

One night, a few months back, Colin accidentally discovered that Meghan had developed a crush on their shared friend. She had just finished reading an email from Sebastien, and before she had fallen asleep, let slip the words, "Goodnight, Sebastien. My love."

Colin had laughed moronically all night long.

Colin was not sure if he had ever seen his sister as mortified, as the night he had discovered she had a crush on Sebastien Jendaya.

The twins pushed their way through the bush and tree filled divider, which separated the campsites, attempting to sneak a peek at the Gypsies.

There was a group of men sitting around a campfire playing strange looking guitars; their fingers moved at incredible speeds, playing music that was catchy, yet soothing, almost trance-like. They looked out of place sitting around a campfire dressed in their brightly colored shirts and winged-tipped shoes.

"Nothing too weird to report here," said Meghan, losing interest. They lingered a minute longer, when something *too* weird did happen.

Colin breathed in abruptly as he lost control of his body and could no longer move. Not even his gaze was under his control. His eyes penetrated another pair of eyes just on the inside of the Gypsy camp.

"Tell me what to do!" he cried silently.

"I don't understand what's happening," Meghan replied, searching his thoughts in vain for something to help her understand.

Colin got a keen sense that someone could clearly see the two of them standing in the woods, spying. His face went white with dread as he saw the shadow of a figure get up and walk in their direction.

"I think I'm going be sick," croaked Colin, trying to look away. His eyes or body would not budge. He remained frozen in place. Being caught spying was definitely not how Colin imagined meeting his new neighbors.

In the next moment, a shrill, screeching howl echoed above them, covering the twins' arms in goose bumps and simultaneously releasing Colin from his statue-like imprisonment.

A sense of panic infiltrated the Gypsy camp, and within seconds, all had disappeared inside the closest wagon.

"How peculiar. It sounded like an owl," said Meghan, her eyes searching the elevated pines. Meghan saw a shadow in Colin's mind and faced the direction he was watching, but saw nothing.

A deep chill brought on a shiver.

After catching the glimpse of the shadow, Colin backed closer to his sister, perplexed at what had occurred. The Gypsy camp was completely deserted.

"What *was* that? I couldn't move," whispered Colin.

Meghan, already shaking off the strange occurrence, seized the opportunity to frighten her brother.

"I'm sure it was a Gypsy cuurrse, to puutt you under their controlll."

"Ha ha, Sis. Very funny," he retorted, not falling for her attempt at frightening him. "Plus, did you notice that they *all* disappeared into *one* wagon?"

"Couldn't have," answered Meghan. "There had to be at least thirty people over there."

"I saw it, and they did," argued Colin.

"Maybe when you weren't looking they all climbed out the back."

Colin did not have time to reply.

"What are you doing in there?" a gruff voice whispered angrily from behind them. They both gasped and spun around. It was Uncle Arnon, who knew exactly what they were doing.

They wondered if perhaps he could also read minds, as he was often a little *too* good at knowing when they were up to trouble.

Arnon stood with arms folded, waiting for an answer.

Colin let Meghan handle the hard part of answering, since he could do little more than tell the truth; which is not the point when caught in the act of something you know will make Uncle Arnon angry.

"We were listening to the music, Uncle Arnon."

"The Gypsies are not outside, so what music?"

"They stopped playing and disappeared inside their wagons," answered Meghan. "Or," she continued, putting on her annoyed face, "if you want to believe the geek patrol, Colin insists they somehow *all* fit themselves into one wagon, after an owl or something screeched overhead. Spooked 'em pretty bad I guess."

"Yeah, imagine being spooked by an owl when you're camping in the middle of the Maine woods," added Colin, unsure of his true feelings on the subject. He was also sure to send Meghan a silent scowl for the *little brother* wisecrack.

Uncle Arnon gawked oddly into the sky, as if expecting to see something. He led the spying duo, by their shoulders, back to the trailer. The twins crossed their eyes at each other, questioning their uncle's unusual behavior.

"I passed the Jendaya site on my way home," he informed them. "They are not quite set up yet, so why don't we have some lunch before you visit."

Meghan pouted in obvious disappointment, but begrudgingly made lunch. An hour later, long after they had finished lunch, the twins began to get the distinct impression that Uncle Arnon was stalling their departure, as he kept them busy doing piddly things around the trailer.

Finally, over an hour later, they noticed a few of the Gypsies were back outside, and once Uncle Arnon had seen this, he told them they could go.

"Behave, please!" he yelled after them. "Come six o'clock, you be at Kanda's fire pit."

They raced across the road and headed into the woods to their secret path (which they had created over the previous six summers), leading to

Sebastien's campsite. Halfway through, they crashed directly into Sebastien.

"'Bout time! I was coming to find you two," he said.

"Sorry, our uncle wouldn't let us go. Besides, he told us you weren't set up yet," Colin said, catching his breath.

"I told your uncle to tell you I was finishing when he passed by."

How strange, thought both twins in confused unison.

"We're together now," said Sebastien. "Whatdyawannado?"

"I'm thirsty, how 'bout a tonic?" said Meghan. "We're almost at The Little Shop anyway, and then we can hang at the lake." They continued on the path, which veered off in two directions; one path lead to the Jendaya camp, and the second, to The Little Shop, which was in the middle of the Cobbscott Campground.

As the trio followed the pathway, an unusual and awkward silence fell over them. Colin sensed Meghan's nerves stopping her from talking, something he rarely had the pleasure to witness. *Can she really have it that bad over Sebastien?* Colin hid the thought from his sister and decided to be nice, by breaking the silence.

"So, it must be nice that schools out?"

"Definitely," agreed Sebastien, glad of the break in tension.

"What about your teams though?" Colin asked. "Don't you miss them in the summer?"

"I suppose a little," admitted Sebastien.

In an artless manner, Meghan finally spoke. "You started telling me in an email about getting to state finals." Even as she blurted it out, she sent a silent glare to Colin that implied, *don't you dare tell him or I will....* She continued seamlessly, adding, "How did that turn out?"

"Oh yeah, I guess I forgot to tell you," and he excitedly went into a story of winning the final big game of the season. After discussing school and sports, Meghan was still abnormally quiet.

"Did you get a look at any of the Gypsy wagons yet, Sebastien?" asked Colin, broaching a new subject.

"No, not yet," he answered.

"Apparently, they're afraid of owls," joked Colin. "They all ran into a wagon, after one screeched."

"*A* wagon?" questioned Sebastien, not missing a beat.

"I'm sure my brother was seeing things, Sebastien. There were too many to fit into one wagon." Meghan was annoyed that Colin was still insisting on this fact.

"That is what I saw, Sis."

"Why don't we go check'em out later?" suggested Sebastien, recalling how the twins' arguments could escalate.

"You two will have to go without me. I'm not spying anymore," announced Colin decidedly.

Sebastien, puzzled, asked, "Why not?"

"Something strange happened, that's why."

For once, Meghan agreed.

"I guess it *was* strange, but still, it's not worth quitting over."

Sebastien waited for an explanation.

Meghan continued.

"Colin and I snuck into the woods to take a peek at the Gypsies, and I think someone caught us."

Colin shuddered at the memory.

"It was as if someone was forcing me to stay where I was. I was frozen in place. Then they all got scared by an owl screeching and ran away." He added, reiterating, "Into one wagon."

"How would that be possible?" asked Sebastien.

"No idea. But even minus that point, our uncle also caught us. So next time, we would be grounded for sure," frowned Colin.

"Nah," said Meghan.

"You don't think so, Sis?"

"Next time we won't get caught, Little Bro."

Also remembering how Meghan's use of the phrase 'little bro' could start a downward spiral in the conversation, Sebastien, thankful they had arrived at The Little Shop, sidetracked the twins.

"We're here. So, tonics all around?"

The twins nodded yes.

The path ended and they came into a clearing behind the tiny camp shop; three people inside would be a crowd and there were already two.

"You wait here, I'll grab the tonics," Colin said, rushing inside, letting the screen door slam behind him.

This left Meghan standing alone with Sebastien, searching her thoughts for something useful to say. *What is wrong with me? I need to get this under control already*, she huffed, silently.

"Yes, you do," a voice echoed in her head.

"Shut up, Col. You are not helping," she shot back.

"Can you at least try not to be weird *all* summer? We wouldn't want to scare away our *only* friend," he sent back sarcastically. To his surprise, he heard her giggle nervously.

"What's so funny?" asked Sebastien. "Did Colin say something funny? Were you doing that talking to each other thing again?" he whispered.

"Sorry, he tripped in the store," she lied.

Meghan sensed Colin frowning.

Sebastien was the only person they had told about their mind-speaking ability, seeing as how one day he figured out something was up and asked them straight out if they could hear each other.

Colin exited with three blueberry tonics, handing one each to Meghan and Sebastien.

Without hesitation, they headed to the edge of Camp Cobbscott, to their favorite spot near the edge

29

of the lake. They sat on an odd shaped tree, which grew sideways rather than up-ways, and spent the afternoon lounging in the shade and wading through the cold water as if the past eight months apart had not even happened. Before they knew it, six o'clock had arrived and they headed to Kanda's fire pit.

Chapter 2

"I can't wait to hear Kanda's new story tonight. I really love her stories," said Colin in a dreamy haze.

Meghan laughed. "You would ya geek!"

Sebastien could not help but laugh, too.

"You don't like them?" Colin asked, perplexed.

"Ah, my nerdy little bro."

Colin cringed at his two least favorite words.

"It's not that I don't like them, per se," she continued, it's just that they always have some point, some moral at the end. They're not just stories."

"So?" Colin replied, still not understanding.

"I think what she's trying to say," said Sebastien, "is that it's too much like learning something."

"It's still a story, though," defended Colin.

"Yes, it is," she agreed. "I have to admit, there's something about Kanda's voice when she tells them, it makes the story seem..." she paused, thinking of the right word.

"Believable," suggested Sebastien.

"Yeah, believable," she agreed. "But it is still too much like learning something, and its summer! I don't want to learn anything unless I have to!"

"That's my sister," thought Colin. "Wouldn't want to learn anything, even by accident."

"I heard that," she snarled aloud, hurrying along to the party.

"What did you hear?" asked Sebastien, but she did not answer. "What did I miss? Were you two using telepathy again?"

"Sorry, Sebastien. It was nothing. Just one of my sister's usual insults."

Colin started running to catch up with her, leaving Sebastien behind, looking confused. He shook his head and followed the twins, muttering, "I'm beginning to hate it when they do that."

A feast ensued with lobster and clam chowder, or as the locals put it, lobstah and chowdah, with ployes for dipping into the chowder, made by Mrs. Jendaya (she makes the best), and loads of fresh corn, potatoes roasted with butter and spices, and biscuits with molasses. For desert, they had another summer evening favorite; blackberry dumplings, served hot with homemade vanilla ice cream. Blackberries were not in season yet, but Kanda always kept some frozen to have throughout the year.

As the incoming night chill set in, the group huddled close to the fire, all eyes lost in the flames, sucked into the designs of the fire.

At precisely nine o'clock, Kanda's voice filtered through the mesmerizing flames and all eyes and ears switched to her. Her voice seemed to mingle with the flames.

"Tonight, I tell a story about truth." She took a calm breath and serenely began.

"Some time ago, there existed a woman whose heart was filled with the desire for power, but the more power she attained the more insatiable her lust became.

Then, by chance, she discovered love; true love, without condition. It changed her, taming her lust for power, and soon, she accepted her new love's proposal of marriage.

Now it was the custom of the day to marry at the rising of the sun, symbolizing the birth of a new beginning, and in the early hours of the long awaited day, a wedding party gathered.

Each member carried a lantern, lit brightly, illuminating their walk to a nearby cliffs edge, where the wedding would take place. Upon arrival, the group dispersed, placing each lantern on the ground, forming a lighted path leading to the bride. The groom would arrive as the last lanterns flame dimmed, which was timed to the rising of the sun.

Finally, the moment arrived. The flame of the final lantern dissolved, just as glorious beams of orange and yellow began to brighten the sky. However, dismay swiftly consumed the wedding party, as the sun's rise finished and the groom did not arrive.

The bride was overwrought with worry. What misfortune had befallen her beloved? Why did he not come?

Immediately a search party dispatched. The others too, believed he had befallen some terrible fate, for they knew he loved this woman, wholeheartedly. Hours passed with no news, when suddenly a young man shouted, 'We found him.'

The bride followed them to a nearby field where a crowd huddled around a body lying on the ground. She froze, fearing the worst.

Then, the body moved and she rushed forward, pushing through the crowd. A man tried to stop the bride, but failed. As soon as she had pushed her way through, she wished the man had succeeded.

She collapsed, clutching her heart.

"This cannot be," she repeated.

The people bowed their heads in shame over the betrayal they each witnessed: the man sleeping in the arms of another woman.

So many things had passed through the woman's head during her beloved's disappearance. Betrayal, however, had not even once crossed her mind.

The man stirred. He saw the woman he should have married earlier that morning and lit up like the sunrise he had missed. Then, as his head became clear, he noticed the woman next to him.

"What is this?" he questioned, pushing her
away. He shook her violently, trying to wake her.
"Who are you?" he questioned.

*He crawled on his knees, begging his true love's
forgiveness. Pleading for a chance to let him
discover the true meaning behind this betrayal; for
in his heart, still filled with love for only her, he
knew that it was no power of his own that brought
him into the arms of this other woman, a complete
stranger.*

*The woman refused any forgiveness or
possibility that there was any other truth other than
what her eyes could see.*

He was her beloved no more.

*Pain and bitterness surged through her veins,
replacing the love she felt for this man.*

*In the weeks that followed, she obsessed over
the agony falling in love had brought her. She lost all
faith in love and vanquished..."* as Kanda said the
word, a torrent of ferocious flame erupted high into
the air and then dissipated. Kanda, looking straight
into the eyes of her hypnotized listeners, continued.

"truth and love from her life."

Kanda closed her eyes, pained by the story.

*"Her old desires for power returned to her nine
fold, and she began a journey from which she could
scarcely return. Her life purpose became to seek
revenge on all those whom she believed had
conspired to make her believe in love.*

The man, her once true love, after months of trying to prove his innocence, finally discovered that he had been poisoned and tricked into the arms of the other woman.

By whom? He did not know. For what purpose? His heart knew the answer. Someone in want of his true love's willingness for greed and power. Someone that knew she would never forgive him.

Unable to bear the burden of this truth, and knowing he would never have the evidence to prove his innocence, the man sent his true love a letter that simply and truthfully stated, 'I will always love you, even beyond my end.' He then went voluntarily into death, jumping from the very cliff on which the couple should have been wed.

The woman, after hearing of his death and reading the letter, felt a flicker of remorse. This remorse was defeated, however, as bitterness filled her shattered heart. Her truth became the final truth! The action of taking his life proved unequivocally that no other truth could exist.

Her life continued, with hatred and greed in place of love and life."

Kanda paused again, this time, casting her gaze directly into the eyes of the twins, sitting side by side.

"Truth is the only real power," she spoke profoundly. *"Truth is freedom. Not pursuing it is a life of captivity!"*

The story ended and everyone remained silent, disappearing once again into the flames of the roaring fire. After a while, Kanda arose and softly offered refills on drinks, and the small party began again to come alive.

"That was an interesting one," said Meghan, a short while later.

"Real happy ending," agreed Sebastien sarcastically.

Colin ignored them, disappearing into his own thoughts, analyzing every word of Kanda's story. There were many holes and unanswered questions. Who had caused the real betrayal and why would they want to cause someone so much pain? Why could the man not prove himself innocent? Though filled with holes, the moral was perfectly clear: Seek the truth, always.

"Hey. Hey. You listening to me, Little Bro?" Meghan interrupted his train of thought.

"*Yes*, I can hear you," he retorted.

"I was trying to tell you that Uncle Arnon said we can stay up past curfew tonight."

Colin checked his watch. It was almost ten already, their normal curfew time.

"It still feels early anyway," he said, pleased at the news.

Excited that the night was not yet ending, he forgot about Kanda's story.

"Don't wander too far, you two," ordered Uncle Arnon.

"Same applies to you, Sebastien," added his father, Milo. They sat close as they could to the fire without being too close to the adults and talked the night away.

Much later that night, as they left the fire pit, Uncle Arnon took the camp road with the Jendayas, leaving the twins and Sebastien at the entrance of the secret path behind The Little Shop. The Jendaya camp was a little closer than the Jacobys', so they left Sebastien at his camp and continued home. The mesmerizing music from the Gypsy camp wafted through the air as they drew closer.

"They seem to be having a good time," whispered Colin. "Let's not go any closer, though," he added, not wanting a repeat of that afternoon.

Before Meghan could answer, a screeching howl ripped through the quiet of the night. A howl that was eerily similar to the one heard earlier that day.

It was much closer this time.

The Gypsy music halted and a huge commotion followed, as once again they scurried into hiding.

For a moment, Colin wanted to watch more closely and see if they all went into one wagon, as before. However, he had an equally strong desire to run and hide.

Uncle Arnon rounded the corner of the camp road just as another screech resonated through the night sky.

"Come on you two, time to get inside," said their uncle, quickening his pace.

"That was the same screech we heard earlier," said Meghan, officially creeped out. "Must be a large owl," she gulped. "I've never heard one like it before."

Shadows danced on the ground around them in what little moonlight streamed through the tall pine trees. Colin jumped as a shadow moved alongside him, but it was just a swaying branch.

"Ha," started Meghan, ready to make fun. In the next second, she froze and sucked in a quick breath. Something unseen beamed a spine-chilling quiver down her back and into Colin's mind. They could not escape the sensation that something unfriendly was watching them, from somewhere close by.

"M-maybe we should hurry?" Colin said, trembling. He did not want to see what was responsible for such a horrific feeling.

As Uncle Arnon led them into the trailer and got them locked up for the night, Meghan's mind raced over the events of the day. Colin sensed this and asked her what she was thinking.

"I hate to admit it, but this whole day seems kind of strange."

"That's an understatement!" he replied. They pondered on the subject for a while, separately, until their uncle's voice intruded into their thoughts.

"Time for bed. Goodnight you two." It was impossible not to notice his hands quivering as he closed their door. The twins crawled into bed, ill by the fact that Uncle Arnon was clearly spooked.

"He's not supposed to be scared of owls, even large ones," Meghan stammered silently.

"It is out of character, but maybe... maybe that screeching isn't an owl. Maybe we missed something. Remember Kanda's story tonight? Always seek the truth, because it might not be what you first think."

"Was that her point? I stopped listening at the end," she lied.

"Yes, it was," he said, shuddering at the thought of some creepy-crawly creature wandering around outside the trailer.

"No. It has to be an owl," she whispered. "I mean, what else could it be?"

Colin shook his head. He had no better answer.

Meghan continued. "What I want to know is why those Gypsies freak out every time that screeching owl, or whatever it is, comes around? And tonight..." she hesitated.

He knew what she was thinking of. Something hidden, something evil, had been watching them. Colin shivered, goosebumps rising on the surface of his skin. His gut told him to hide, but if he crawled any deeper into his bed covers, he would soon be sleeping at the foot of his bed.

"That was pretty creepy," agreed Meghan, again hating to admit that it had frightened her. Then, attempting to lesson their level of alarm, she added, "It was the middle of the night! Which is always creepy here."

"True," he agreed. "However, owls don't typically screech during the day, and the first time we heard it was this afternoon, in broad daylight," he reminded.

"It's always dark in the woods! Maybe it messes with their day and night radar!"

The conversation ended with Meghan rolling over and facing the wall. She hid her true feelings from her brother, so as not to frighten him more than he already was. More so, she had a nagging feeling that the screeching howls had something to do with the Gypsies. Come tomorrow, she was determined to find out why.

Unbeknownst to her, Colin was having a similar hidden thought, however, slightly altered. *How come I have a feeling Meghan's going to be dragging me along to spy on those Gypsies, again?* He tried to put the thought and the day out of his mind, pulled the covers over his head, and eventually fell asleep.

Meghan found herself dreaming in no time.

She skipped through the woods hand in hand with Sebastien. He did not speak, but simply smiled his hypnotizing smile. Fog covered their path suddenly and Sebastien tripped, letting go of her hand, vanishing into the fog.

Meghan, now alone, fought through the thick fog trying to find her way. She panted heavily, losing her breath. Poisonous fumes threatened to fill her lungs. She realized she was not breathing fog, but smoke!

A silhouette emerged from the smoke. Meghan shouted for help. The figure was holding a handkerchief over its face. As it came closer, Meghan realized it was Colin.

"How did I get here? Am I in your dream, for real?" he asked, dragging his sister lower to the ground, hoping for clearer air.

Meghan started to panic. It was the most life-like dream she had ever had, and now, Colin was stuck in here with her. She kept repeating to herself that it was only a dream.

Colin motioned for her to follow. Surprised at his relative calmness, she crawled behind him. Soon, scorching heat replaced the smoke. It forced them to stop crawling and stand up.

Twenty feet in front of them a tree burned, smoke billowing from the top, and to the twins' horror, a young girl sat in one of the branches, appearing not to care that fire was about to engulf her.

"This is only a dream," panted Meghan.

"Of course it is," agreed Colin, beginning to lose his nerve.

Meghan took a step closer, ignoring the urge to scream at the girl, and instead calmly coaxed her.

"Hey, little girl, you should get down from there."

The pale faced girl stared down at them from her perch. Her deep-red, nearly black hair shifted in the fire's wake. Her eyes never left contact with

Meghan's, but her arm raised and pointed. The twins' gazes turned and focused on where she was pointing. A moving ball of fire blustered toward them. Meghan twisted in circles searching desperately for a safe passage out of this fiery mess but the fire and smoke were too thick.

"What is that?" asked Colin sharply.

"I must wake up. Please someone wake me up."

"Yes," agreed Colin, "Please someone, wake you up!" He clasped her hand in his but instantly let go, covering his head instead, in attempt to protect it from the ball of flame gliding closer.

Meghan turned away.

Colin muttered desperately, "Wake up already!"

"Still no idea how to accomplish that feat," she yelled back, at the same time noticing that the little girl in the tree had disappeared.

"Hey, the little girl, she's go..." Meghan did not complete her sentence as Colin gasped and made a small, half attempt at a tug on her arm.

Colin stood beside her, his eyes wide with fear. Meghan turned around, one slow step at a time, afraid of what she would see.

There in front of her, staring back through the ball of flame was Meghan. She froze, horrified, as she watched the other her engulfed by the flames. Although the other her did not seem to be in any pain.

Meghan could not believe what she was seeing! Her image edged closer, extending her burning arm. Meghan backed away, shaking.

"Colin!" she called out.

There was no answer. She hastily glanced around. He was gone.

The on fire Meghan was nearly engulfing the real Meghan, who discovered she had backed into a tree. A voice, her voice, echoed out of the flames.

"Do not be afraid. These flames will protect you."

"Protect me from what? The only thing I need protection from is you. Oh why can't I wake up?" she said, exasperated.

The flames thrashed at her skin, but to her amazement, they did not burn her. She closed her eyes, waiting to feel herself burning alive in her own dream.

When she finally dared open them, the second Meghan was gone and she alone stood with the flames engulfing her. She stretched out her arms examining the flames licking at her skin, amazed that they did not burn. Even more confusing was that the flames felt like a protective shield that coated her entire body.

"This is by far, the strangest dream I have ever, *ever* had!"

Meghan jumped, startled, when the little girl suddenly appeared in front of her. She held out her hand to touch Meghan.

"No, you'll hurt yourself," screamed Meghan, backing away. The girl laughed, her own hand bursting into flame.

"Now, I am no longer alone," she said playfully. "I am sorry, though," she added, her face turning sour.

"Sorry?" questioned Meghan, confused.

"For what comes next," she whispered gravely.

A speechless Meghan watched as flames engulfed the girls' body, and seconds later, her silhouette dissolved into the smoke and flame, leaving Meghan alone.

Meghan closed her eyes again, this time hearing voices in the distance, calling her. Her mind followed them and when she opened her eyes, she was awake and on the floor of her bedroom, drenched in sweat. Uncle Arnon knelt on the floor next to her, with Colin beside him, looking half frightened to death.

Meghan struggled to find her voice, asking for water. Colin ran for a glass. Her uncle helped her sit up and examined her arms and legs.

"What are you looking for?" she managed to ask, still catching her breath. She wondered if Colin had told him about the dream. Then, she wondered if Colin had actually been there at all.

"You fell off the bed, just making sure nothings broken. Must have been some dream. You okay?"

"Yeah, except, I feel kind of beat up." Every muscle in her body ached, and flames still burned hot in her mind.

Colin arrived with the water.

"I made it *extra* cold."

It was hint enough to confirm that he had indeed been stuck in her dream. After making sure she was not physically injured, Arnon sighed, relieved, and then ordered the twins back to bed. As soon as their uncle was back in his own bed, she sat up.

"Colin," she said through her thoughts.

"Are your dreams always that fun?" he asked her.

"Very funny, Col. It was so real. I never have such vivid dreams. You disappeared. What happened?"

"Uncle Arnon woke me. You had fallen off the bed and he came running in. You were flopping around having some sort of seizure or something."

She wrinkled her nose at the thought of wobbling around on the floor uncontrollably as others watched.

"What happened after I left the dream?" Colin asked cautiously, unsure he wanted to hear it.

"The flames overtook me, the other Meghan disappeared and I became her, in the flames. Strange part is, the fire didn't burn me. And then, the little girl came back and said…" she hesitated.

"What, what did she say?" Colin asked impatiently.

"She said, 'I am no longer alone' and something about being sorry about something." It was starting to become fuzzy in Meghan's memory.

"What does that mean?"

"How do I know?" she snapped back, silently.

"Sorry." He waited for her to continue.

"If I had to, Col, I'd swear it really happened."

"I would say its official now, we have been at camp for a hardly a day and already it's the strangest summer we have ever had."

Meghan could not argue with that fact.

"I'm tired now," she muttered. "Night, Col. Going back to sleep."

"Okay, and a, no more dreams, or at least, leave me out of it, huh?"

She did not reply, and secretly hoped it would never happen again. She tossed and turned, the dream refusing to leave her thoughts, the heat of the flames still nagging at her subconscious. With each passing minute aggravation kept her from falling asleep and annoyance replaced confusion and concern.

Colin also had trouble falling back to sleep. His thoughts reeled through various topics, but none more so than how he had ended up in his sister's dream. He must have hooked onto her thoughts while they were sleeping. It had never happened before, but their ability had changed over the years, so why not again?

Then, an alarm went off in his head. How would they control this new ability if it happened while they were sleeping? Would and could this happen every night?

It was a devastating thought. Not only because of the interruption in their sleep, or being forced to participate in his sister's dreams, but that his dreams were the one place no one, including his mind-reading sister, could ever get into. It was his only safe place. The only place he was completely free.

He could not allow it to happen again!

"How do I stop it, though?" he whispered. "How do I control something that happens while I'm sleeping?" Unsure of how to control this new step in their abilities, he attempted to clear his mind, hoping it would be enough. He tossed and turned, pulling the covers over his head, and waited impatiently for sleep.

Sebastien arrived the next morning and the trio headed to the lake, not too far from their favorite sideways growing tree. They looked forward to a morning boat trip. In minutes, they arrived and found Kanda's boat, tied up at a dock near the shore.

"It might take all morning just to get that knot out," said Colin, sighing.

"Nah! I can get it out in no time!" Sebastien promised, setting in to untying the mess of rope that was keeping the boat attached to the dock. After fifteen minutes, he had made little progress, and the trio's excitement waned.

A presumptuous voice startled them from behind.

"I could help you with that," the voice called out.

A boy the twins recognized, as the dangly haired Gypsy boy they had made eye contact with, leaned against a tree, with his arms loosely crossed.

The trio gawked awkwardly at the scrawny boy, but did not answer.

"Okay," the boy said smugly. "Do you not need any help, then?"

"Sorry," said Meghan. "You startled us."

"It's just that, I'm pretty good with knots," the Gypsy boy continued.

"I can't seem to make any progress," said Sebastien, stepping aside. "Be my guest," he said, motioning for the boy to give a try.

The boy knelt down, first looking over the knot, then hid the rope from view. Just a minute later he stood up, rope in hand. The stunned trio clapped their hands, astounded at how dexterously he had done it.

"Wow! Thanks!" said Meghan, smiling at the boy.

"Was nothing," the boy insisted.

"My name is Meghan by the way, and that is my brother, *my twin brother*, Colin. And this is our friend Sebastien."

"That's cool, name's Jae. I'm staying in the camp too. You might have noticed all the wagons."

"Yeah, we saw them," piped in Colin. "We were eating breakfast when you guys arrived in the camp. I really like the music you play on those strange looking guitars, too." Colin realized he had said a mouthful and was afraid he had given away the fact that they had been spying. His face turned beet red and he cast his gaze to the ground.

The Gypsy boy did not seem to care.

"We were about to paddle around the lake. Would you care to join us, Jae?" asked Meghan.

His gaze shifted back and forth between the campground and the boat, apparently struggling with the decision.

"Okay, I'll come," he finally answered. "But I can't stay out for too long." Sadness replaced any smugness in his voice. Then almost as instantly, the sadness disappeared.

"How about I paddle?" he suggested as they hopped in. "I haven't had the chance in ages."

The twins certainly did not mind. This meant they could sit back and enjoy the ride, as they knew Sebastien would insist on taking the second paddle.

They shoved off from the dock, heading toward the middle of the lake. The water was clear and cool, with patches of fog still rolling off the surface, fighting to survive as the sun rose higher in the sky. Minnows swam near the surface, toying with the lake spiders as they glided across, leaving tiny waves of water in their wake.

Colin sat in the middle of the boat, with Jae in the front, leaving Meghan and Sebastien sharing the back seat. Meghan watched him row, thinking to herself how well he did it. Every motion was smooth and effortless. She did not linger in her daydream long however, as Colin broke in, teasingly.

"You like Sebastien. You like Sebastien."

Meghan's temper was instantly hot, but she ignored him.

After awhile, chirps and buzzing, from frogs, insects and birds, replaced the rolling fog. Thankfully, the sun beaming down frightened away the mosquitoes. Otherwise, they would have spent the entire day swatting instead of paddling or relaxing.

"So, we heading in any particular direction?" asked Jae, after they reached the lake's center.

"My votes for the marshes," said Sebastien. "Sometimes there's large lake turtles in there."

"Turtles?" questioned Jae tensely. "How large exactly?"

"I've seen a couple close to two feet," boasted Sebastien.

The smugness returned, with Jae's under-his-breath reply, which none of the three could decipher.

"What was that, Jae?" asked Meghan.

"Hope we get to see one," he stated, clearly not repeating what he had actually said.

"Be careful as we get closer, it's easy to get tangled in the plants," Sebastien warned.

Jae signaled back, okay.

Meghan lifted her hand out of the water, which had been skimming the surface, having no desire to feel slimy plants against her skin.

"So, Jae," she started, "where is your caravan from?"

Colin was glad she had finally asked, seeing as he had wanted to, but had not dared.

Jae answered the question as if he had rehearsed the answer a hundred times.

"Traveling is our life. We are not from any *one* place."

"Have you always traveled around? Because we have since we were two, with our uncle," explained Colin, growing more comfortable with the new stranger.

"I can't believe you would do so by choice," said a clearly baffled Jae. "Wouldn't you rather live in just one place?" Disbelief now replaced the arrogance in Jae's voice. Then, again, he changed his mind. "I mean, I can understand why your uncle would choose to travel, there really is no better way to live."

Meghan, Colin and Sebastien were mystified by Jae's incessant turns in attitude. Colin explained his own position on the subject.

"Cobbscott is the only place we visit for any real length of time; four entire months every summer. It is definitely my favorite place, but living here year round would not be fun at all. Once the campground closes for winter, the town shuts down. It would be quite boring, cold and snowy. Mostly, though, I like traveling because that means Uncle Arnon is my teacher, and I do not have to attend normal school."

"Definitely right on that count!" agreed Meghan, adding, "I have no idea how people survive real school. Although, I suppose one day it might be nice to live in just one place, when I'm older maybe. Can't imagine where I'd want to live, though."

The conversation ended and the rowing ceased as the boat came to a slow stop. The foursome listened and watched for anything interesting in the water, the surface of which was still and glass-like. Colin noticed that all the minnows and lake spiders had disappeared.

"Ah let's go! This is boring," blurted out Meghan after too many minutes of nothing. They all agreed.

Sebastien and Jae started to paddle, but the boat refused to move.

"What's going on?" asked a frustrated Sebastien.

They searched the water below, anxiously. A low moan echoed from underneath the boat. Meghan sat down, grasping her seat.

"What was that?" she muttered.

"Nothing to worry about, I'm sure," reassured Sebastien, still looking over the boat's edge, alongside Colin.

"We need to get free!" yelled Jae, suddenly sounding panicked.

Meghan, Colin and Sebastien started to reach Jae's level of panic when bubbles of foamy water began surging up the sides of the boat. The surge splashed Colin's face, which daringly still dangled over the boat's edge.

"There's something down there," he said, stumbling sideways as he tried to sit back down.

"Grab him!" shouted Meghan. "He's gonna tip the boat!" Jae gently lunged forward and steadied Colin, stabilizing the boat.

Sebastien picked up his paddle and attempted to get the boat moving. Jae joined him, but the boat did not budge.

Colin stood back up and from a more distant vantage point, carefully looked into the water. More bubbles burst to the surface. "There *is* something down there!" he insisted, plunking down onto his seat.

"What exactly do you mean by something down there?" asked Jae, with growing agitation.

"Look for yourselves!" Colin challenged, gripping the edge of the boat, hoping not to fall out.

"There's nothing in these waters, it's a lake," argued Sebastien.

"Just telling you what I saw," said Colin, determined not to move from his seat.

Meghan sat next to Sebastien, her eyes peering over the edge, afraid she might actually see something down in the water, but was straight back in her seat when the boat began rocking violently.

The moaning below the boat resonated so much that it felt as though the boat might vibrate into shreds. More bubbles escaped to the surface, boiling around the walls of the boat. Sebastien and Jae stopped paddling. They needed all their strength just to stay seated.

Jae looked as if he might be sick.

"This is my fault," he mumbled. "I shouldn't have come." No one responded. They were too frightened to care what Jae meant.

The boat began to rise up out of the lake. Water seeped in through a crack forming in the bottom. Meghan screamed and fell into Sebastien's lap as the boat lurched to the side. There was no time for embarrassment over falling into his lap, as seconds later, the four passengers were tossed out of the boat and into the frigid, slimy-plant and leech-filled water.

Meghan and Sebastien surfaced beside each other, looking more plant-like than human. Meghan choked on a slimy weed that found its way into her mouth.

Jae had already started swimming to shore.

Sebastien helped Meghan clear the tangle of plants surrounding her and they followed Jae.

A voice rang out in Meghan's mind. "Sis," it called, hesitantly.

"Colin!" She sensed fear in her brother's mind and swam faster. Sebastien made it to shore with Meghan right behind. He started to help her out of the water when his hand dropped, his eyes widened and his mouth fell open.

"I know I look like crap right now, but give a girl a break, huh!"

Sebastien could not speak. He could only point over her head, at the lake. She stood at the waters edge and turned around.

"Impossible!" she whispered, nearly falling back into the water. The boat was broken, split down the middle and partly sunken, with Colin sitting upright, seemingly on the surface of the water.

"I've landed on it," he whispered ominously, pointing below the surface.

"Keep very still," said Jae with growing unease.

"How do we get him out?" cried Meghan.

The water around Colin began to bubble again.

"Grab onto something," ordered Sebastien.

"What would you suggest I grab onto exactly," Colin shouted.

Something began to surface, lifting Colin completely out of the water.

A monstrous set of antlers appeared, covered in lake plants, followed by a massive muscular body.

Colin straddled the animal's back. It had to be seven feet tall, the antlers nearly six feet wide.

Recognition seemed to hit everyone at once.

It was a moose, just a moose.

"I should've known," Sebastien said, relieved. "What else that big would be underneath the water around here?" The moose continued chomping on food, unnoticing of the boy sitting on its back or the youngsters standing on the shore.

"At least the sun is still shining," he added. "Gonna be a long walk back home!" His laughter tripled as he helped the slime and now leech covered Meghan onto the bank. She pulled him back into the water for it, and then once on the bank, started pulling off leeches, grumbling with each new one she found.

Jae fell onto the ground, rolling and laughing, seeming the most relieved of all. He bounced off the ground and swam back out to assist Colin, keeping his distance so as not to startle the moose.

"I think it's best to wait for it to go back under, and slowly slide off its back and into the water, Colin. It doesn't even notice you're there. You'll be fine."

"Easy for you to say," replied Colin doubtfully, while clinging onto the antlers to keep steady. "You're not sitting atop a seven foot tall moose!"

They waited, while the moose, still acting quite unaware of the human presence, munched on a lake plant. After a few minutes, it shifted itself around and began to sink under the water.

"I'm not a strong swimmer," Colin reminded the group, as the moose took him even farther from shore.

"You'll be fine. Do what Jae said. Let go and slide into the water," his sister urged.

"Remember to kick your legs once you're in the water," added Sebastien. Colin cautiously slipped off the moose and tried to maneuver his body so that he was heading toward the shore. Jae swam out and helped him. Once in shallow water Jae let go and they collapsed onto the bank, out of breath, and covered in leeches.

"Unbelievable," Jae said to the other three. "I've seen a lot of things, but that was definitely different."

"I've heard stories about moose surfacing next to people out fishing before," said Meghan, "But to actually see it…"

"I think what happened here might be a first!" Sebastien told her.

The echoes of their laughter carried across the once again calm water.

Meghan helped Colin sit up, and set in to peeling off his leeches.

"Man these things find blood fast," said Jae, finally plucking off his last one.

As they slogged back around the lake looking for an exit that would take them to the road, the twins could not help but notice that Jae's mood had improved, as they laughed and relived the moose adventure.

The rest of the day passed quickly and in the late afternoon, the chill of evening rolled in along with patches of fog. Meghan shivered. They had finally come out of the woods, but there was still a good distance to go. Jae ran up to her and offered his somewhat dry jacket. He kept walking, not waiting for any response.

"Thanks," she said, lingering her eye on him.

"Too bad we can't get fully dry," said Sebastien, regaining her attention.

"Hm. Oh, yeah. I know. This humidity sucks. You can't get anything dry in this weather." They continued trudging down the road hoping a driver would come by, but it did not look recently used, as overgrown plants attempted to take over the open space. Late afternoon passed into evening and soon, it was nearly dark.

The later and darker it became, the more Jae's attention turned to the sky. Unease grew noticeably in his eyes.

"What are you looking for?" asked Meghan. *Maybe we can find out more about those screeching, howly things.*

Jae stalled for a minute but finally answered.

"Nothing. Nothing at all. Just not fond of the dark," he insisted.

The twins could not help but notice that his pace continued to pick up though, the closer they got to the campground.

Many long hours after the moose ordeal had ended, they found themselves, at last, at the camp's entrance. As they neared the Jacoby camp Jae stopped once again, standing with his arms folded.

"It was an interesting day," Jae said. "But I gotta run." A bit of the arrogance returned as he hurried away.

"Wait," said Meghan, handing him back his jacket. "Thanks again for that. If you don't get into too much trouble, maybe you could hang out again tomorrow."

Jae stammered for a moment, apparently taken aback by the request.

"Wish I could, guys. It's been great to spend the day with you all, but, you see, we are leaving tomorrow night, and I'll have to help with the preparations." He shrugged, then waved goodbye, vanishing around the corner before they could respond.

"And just like that, he's gone," said Colin somberly. Meghan wondered if Jae's apparent arrogance was blocking the same feeling she and Colin always felt: people never stay around too long, so why get to know them.

"We need to get home," reminded Sebastien, after a quiet moment. "Everyone's probably going nuts worrying about where we are."

The twins rolled their eyes knowing he was right. The trio scurried toward the Jacoby campsite.

As expected, a group had gathered at Arnon's trailer. Four figures rushed them with instant questions and sighs of relief.

"Where on earth have you been?" demanded Uncle Arnon, standing next to Kanda Macawi. "You were due home hours ago! We were about to put together a search party!"

"Why are you all covered in mud?" asked Sebastien's mother, when Arnon finally took a breath.

The three took turns explaining, each filling in parts left out by the other, including meeting Jae.

"I'm surprised you didn't see him run by," said Colin. "He was right ahead of us." The adults shook their heads. None of them had seen Jae.

With the adventure fully explained, the adults now laughed as hard as the youngsters had after the event had occurred, possibly harder.

"We will grab you some dinner. You must be starved," said Kanda, as she motioned Sebastien's mother, Kay, to follow her into the kitchen.

Uncle Arnon fell into a chair, still in disbelief. Sebastien's father, Milo, patted Arnon's shoulder, and set to lighting a fire.

The twins, as exhausted as they were, could not help but feel the pat on the shoulder had some hidden meaning they did not understand. Especially when after a minute, Arnon disappeared into the trailer and hushed whispers escaped an open window.

The twins grew more suspicious when Milo ordered them all closer to the fire, to warm up. The fire pit was too far away to overhear what they were discussing inside the trailer. The hidden conversation did not last long however, as minutes later they exited, serving dinner.

Once warmed and fed, the Jacoby's guests decided to head home. After a round of goodnights, the twins watched as the Jendayas and Kanda Macawi faded into the night.

"I think we should make it an early night tonight," their uncle said, while putting out the fire. "You guys look exhausted."

"I am pretty tired. I think I'll clean up first though," said Meghan. She sauntered into the trailer. A moment later Uncle Arnon and Colin jumped as Meghan let out a scream.

"What is it? Are you hurt?" asked her uncle, worried there was some overlooked injury.

"Why did someone not tell me how terrible I look?"

Both the Jacoby men rolled their eyes.

"We did fall into a lake, Sis. Remember?"

Meghan did not hear him. She was too concerned with pulling mud-caked weeds from her tangled hair and washing the dark streaked makeup off her face.

"Ahhh!" she then screamed, again. "Get it off me!" she demanded, pointing at her hairline. "Get it off! Get it off! Get it off!"

"Well stand still so I can see," ordered her uncle.

Colin's stomach turned when a second later Arnon located the object of her horror.

"That sure is a doozy!" he said, gently plucking a severely blood-bloated leech from her forehead. He opened the trailer door and heaved it into the woods, being sure to wash his hands afterward.

Colin washed his too. He had not touched it, but he had been close enough.

Meghan proceeded to grow more agitated by the minute and disappeared into the bathroom. Before showering, she did a full body search for any lingering bloodsuckers. Thankfully, she found none.

After bathing she rested at the kitchen table, make-up-less, losing herself in a thought. She sipped on hot blackberry cider, a specialty of her uncle's.

Colin took his turn in the bathroom. After finding the still attached leech on Meghan, his uncle had done a search on him but found nothing. Colin did a once over in the shower, just to be sure.

Back in the kitchen, Arnon sat across the table, watching Meghan intently, trying to grasp what she could possibly be thinking. He called her name, but she did not hear him.

"Meghan," he said loud enough to catch her mind.

"Sorry, d'you say something?"

"I was wondering about your dream last night. Wondering, actually, if that has ever happened to you before?"

Meghan had almost forgotten about the previous night's fiery dream, and the hairs on her skin felt instantly singed at the mere memory of it.

"It was some stupid dream about me and Colin, and another little girl, who was caught in a fire."

"A fire. That would be scary." He lifted his eyebrows, leaning forward.

"And was that the first time you and Colin have ever shared a dream?" he asked intently.

Meghan gasped, speechless! She imagined her face must have given away how stunned she was, because her uncle continued without waiting for an answer.

"Sorry, didn't mean to frighten you. You did not honestly think I wasn't aware of your talent did you? What kind of uncle would I be if I hadn't seen it many years ago?"

"How long ago did you figure it out?" she stammered.

"Not long after you came to live with me, actually. You were both so little, then," he reminisced. "You probably don't remember this, but the two of you had this special language you spoke, just between the two of you. I could never understand what you were saying. But then one day, about a year later, you just stopped.

"I noticed little things after that. One or the other of you would respond to a question, or joke, and I was quite certain I had heard nothing said from the other. I caught on pretty quick." He winked at Meghan.

"You're right, Uncle Arnon. I do not remember that at all. I really don't even remember the exact moment that Colin and I realized we were different, and that not everyone could speak to each other through their minds, like we could." She paused and added, "I'm sorry we never told you about it. I guess it seems silly now. We always thought you might be angry, or think we were freaks or something."

"Freaks! Never!" he insisted. "And do not be sorry, either. I have always been impressed with the way you two kept the secret. And believe me, there are people out there that would unfortunately think you are freaks."

Meghan nodded in agreement.

"So," Arnon continued. "Was that the first time sharing a dream?" he asked again.

"Yeah, it was. Why do you ask? And how *did* you know Col was in my dream?"

"Curiosity mostly, wondering how your talent will develop. And Colin was clearly spooked, I sort of assumed," he chuckled, adding more seriously, "You haven't told anyone else about your secret have you?"

"Only Sebastien," she answered honestly, with a tinge of guilt. "He kind of guessed one day, a couple of summers ago. Don't worry, though! He has never told anyone else."

"I assumed as much," Arnon replied knowingly.

Meghan still had the look of shock on her face as Colin came out of the shower. His eyes darted back and forth between them.

"What?" He reached for his head. "Did I forget to rinse the shampoo from my hair again?"

"Would you prefer to do the honor or should I?" Meghan asked amusingly. Uncle Arnon put out his hand in a gesture for her to go ahead.

"Our secret," she announced, "is out!"

Colin fell backwards, his towel nearly falling off. After regaining his composure, he stood with the same flummoxed expression as Meghan had had, only minutes before.

"Don't worry, Col. He figured us out ages ago, even before we did."

"I thought we hid it pretty well," said Colin.

"That's what I thought, too," replied Meghan dryly. She sent Colin a transcript of the last few minutes' conversation. Arnon seemed to understand this and gave them time to finish.

"To be honest," started Arnon, when it looked as though they were finished, "I've heard of twins having a secret language only each other can understand, but, I think you guys are a little different, so…"

"So we shouldn't go telling people about it," guessed Colin.

Arnon smiled. "Since Sebastien knows, that's fine. He's a good friend, and I do not think it's something he would ever use against you."

"Sebastien, never," Meghan defended. "Besides, what do Colin or I have, that people could hold over us, other than telepathy?" she added sarcastically.

Seeing her uncle's concerned face she continued.

"We will, of course, be careful regardless. Because like you said, not everyone is as cool and understanding as you are." She got up and gave her uncle a quick hug. Before she could let go, Arnon gave them one last warning.

"I know you are both careful, but just remember that both Sebastien and I guessed, so others could, too."

"We will do our best, Uncle Arnon," insisted Colin.

Meghan nodded in agreement.

Colin joined Meghan for a hot blackberry cider before heading to bed. It was a relief to have their secret out in the open; they had always felt guilty for not telling their uncle, but had honestly feared the consequences.

Meghan finished her cider, moved a load of laundry from the washer to the dryer, emptied the trash, and then washed up a few dirty dishes. As she finished, Colin dropped his empty mug in the sink. She frowned, deciding to leave it there until morning.

"Off to bed now both of you, long day tomorrow."

"Long day?" they asked in confused unison. Their uncle stuttered for a second then changed his phrasing.

"What I meant to say is, it has been a long day today, and we all have a whole new day to get through tomorrow, which will be longer than today if we do not get our rest, after a long exhausting day like today."

The twins eyed him, untrustingly, but went off to bed.

"Are you starting to get the feeling that Uncle Arnon is up to something?" asked Meghan.

"Maybe he was nervous about admitting he knew our secret."

"Yeah, probably. Or maybe it's our birthday party!" squealed Meghan, instantly sidetracked by the idea of presents. "I wonder what he's planning?"

"Night, Sis," sighed Colin. He could sense by her wandering thoughts that discussing any topic other than birthday presents would be a useless endeavor.

"Yeah, night, Col," she whispered back. She fell asleep minutes later dreaming of what wonderful gifts Sebastien would buy her.

Meghan's excitement leaked into Colin's subconscious while sleeping. He opened the block, just a little, allowing her happiness to envelop him. It was a pleasant way to fall asleep.

Shortly after, Colin jumped awake, remembering the previous night's fiery dream.

"No. I have to keep the block in place! No repeats of last night!" he said, determined. "We have to keep our dreams to ourselves, if nothing else."

Chapter 3

Meghan and Colin waited at the secret path's edge for Sebastien. It was the first day of the Blue Moon Festival, which only took place during a summer that happened to have two full moons in one month. Mainly, the festival attracted tourists, but locals could often be spotted weaving through the crowds, too. It was a grand festival, with food, music, a flea market (Colin's favorite) and a few old carnival rides no one was ever sure were safe to ride, but did anyway.

While they waited for Sebastien, the twins wandered down the camp road toward the Gypsy camp, hoping to catch Jae and say goodbye one last time. He was nowhere in sight.

Footsteps scraped across the gravel behind them. Hoping it was Sebastien, they spun around, but rather than their friend, the twins were accosted by two tall stacks of packages. In attempts to avoid crashing into the twins, the two people carrying the packages jumped out of the way, causing the packages to fall and scatter all over the camp road.

An older, stern-faced and unfamiliar boy stood by a familiar one; the familiar face began anxiously picking up his scattered packages.

"Hey guys, sorry," said Jae, sounding distressed.

"It's a wonder you could walk at all, carrying all that," said Meghan.

"Let us help you the rest of the way," insisted Colin, already picking up a package.

The unknown boy, dressed in a casual sports jacket, had already picked up his packages and was leaving Jae behind, eying him sternly as he walked by, but never saying a word.

His eyes grazed Meghan's and she instantly found that she hated him. Could she really know this, so soon after meeting someone?

"Is that boy always so friendly?" asked Meghan, as he disappeared.

"Ivan? He's not so much unfriendly, as all about business."

"All about business?" questioned Colin.

"Hates wasting time, always working, that sorta thing."

Meghan offered again to help him back to his campsite.

"No!" he replied hastily. "I mean, thanks, but I got it."

"Are you sure? 'Cause it's no bother," she said.

"No, I'll be fine. I gotta hurry, though. They will be expecting me back by now."

The twins piled the last packages back onto Jae's arms.

"I hope you didn't get into trouble yesterday for getting home so late," said Colin.

"Yesterday?" he appeared deep in thought. "Oh, that. Uh, it was okay."

The twins were pleased they had not caused him any trouble.

"Sorry I can't hang longer," he added tiredly. "So many things to do today." He trudged toward his campsite. "Maybe our path'll cross again sometime."

"Yeah, maybe," shouted Colin.

"Good luck, wherever you go next," Meghan shouted.

"Thanks. Same to you," Jae echoed back.

"Wonder where they are heading with such a big group?" she asked.

"Can't imagine," replied Colin. "It must be a ton of work. It's a lot with only you, me, and Uncle Arnon. There must be two hundred of them all together."

Sebastien materialized from the secret path. "Hey guys."

"Finally," said the twins in unison.

"Sorry. Got held up helping my dad with something."

The twins forgot about Jae and his caravan, and the trio headed into town. Their uncle and the Jendayas were going to join them later.

It was about a mile walk down a winding country road, which opened up to a sunny clearing about half way to the town. The thick pines gave way to birches and maples, surrounded by vast, blueberry bush covered fields. The surface of the lake shimmered in the distance as the trio walked passed a graveyard, which indicated their arrival into the town of Cobbscott, Maine.

Music streamed through the breeze, followed by the hum of a crowd behind it. They quickened their pace, and Meghan, wanting to make sure her hair and clothes were just right, said aloud, by accident, "Hope I look okay." She did not get the response she expected.

"I think you look great!" said Sebastien, grinning. "Sorry, you weren't talking to me, were you?" he realized.

Colin did not wait for the two of them to get over their awkwardness. He continued onward, making a nasty face at Meghan as he passed by.

"Not exactly," admitted Meghan, blushing. "But, thanks."

"I meant what I said. You always look great! Though, I'm especially partial to when you wear slimy lake plants and leeches in your hair."

She humpfed and hit him in the shoulder. They hurried to catch up with an outwardly annoyed Colin.

As soon as they were in Cobbscott, they went directly to the music. A rock band played, so they listened and danced. After a full set of music, Colin sent Meghan a thought saying he was bored and was going to the flea market. She noticed agitation in his voice.

"We'll find you later, okay?" she said. Meghan sensed him throwing angry thoughts at her and said, "Now what?"

Sebastien threw a questioning gaze her direction.

"Oh, not you. Colin, mad at me again."

"For what? Something I couldn't hear you guys arguing about?" he asked, slightly miffed.

"Well, yes and no." She stalled, not wanting to admit, *we were fighting over your attention.*

"Anything you want to share?" he prodded. His handsome eyes peeled into the layers of her skin and she nearly let the truth fly.

"I think we should just go find Colin," she mustered out. "I have a feeling he might get into trouble. Those same bullies are around and *I'm the only one...*"

"*Who gets to bully my little brother...* I haven't forgotten, Meghan." He asked curiously, "Why do you call him your little brother anyway? Isn't he technically older than you by a few minutes?"

"He's small," she shrugged. "An easy target for trouble. He always needs my help."

"Don't you think you should stop sticking up for him so much? I mean, what would happen if you were not around? It's bound to happen."

Meghan stared at him, baffled. He was talking like a grown up.

"Why would I not be around?" she asked testily.

"It's always a possibility. You're not going to be fourteen forever, things change."

"I'm not fourteen yet, I'm turning thirteen next week, remember?" She was getting upset now. How could he forget how old she was? "Let's just go find Colin," she said. "He enjoys spending time with you. You are the big brother he'll never have." She rolled her eyes as if her brother was intruding on her life.

Sebastien followed, dropping the subject.

They found Colin deep in the flea market, in a tent far away from the others. It was full of old books, antiques, and knickknacks that seemed to have no purpose.

"Hey guys," he beamed. He had not expected them to find him. He pointed to a tattered looking old man behind the counter. His long hair was white, and pulled back in a ponytail and he leaned on a cane.

"This is Jasper Thorndike. He owns all of this."

The man nodded hello.

They waited patiently, as Jasper showed Colin around the store. Meghan and Sebastien were only partially listening, but tried to act interested. On more than one occasion, they caught each other's eye and tried not to laugh.

They were finally about to leave when Colin stopped to browse over some books he had missed.

At that same moment, Jasper Thorndike came out from behind the counter. He spoke with a grizzled voice.

"I can't help but notice that you like my books."

"I would take them all if I could," Colin responded.

"Don't you have enough already?" argued Meghan.

He ignored her, his eyes glued to an antique velvet-covered book the white-haired man pulled out of his vest. Jasper set it gently on the counter, pronouncing the title, seeing that Colin was not sure how to.

"Magi-cantee…magic and then antee…like ante up, put together."

"Magicante," Colin repeated, enthralled.

Meghan and Sebastien glanced over his shoulder and watched as he opened it, carefully.

"Wow, what are these?" Colin asked Jasper.

"A collection, a pretty darn good one, and one I would only entertain selling to the right buyer."

Inside the book was a collection of thickly textured exotic leaves, colored in deep browns and reds, with glimmers of gold. They measured four to five inches wide, and were equally long. Meghan could see that Colin would not leave without the book. He loved collections and this one was unique.

"These aren't from around here, are they?" he asked, captivated. Deeper in, the leaves glimmered with yellows, greens and silver.

"No, I dare say they are not! However, I am not at liberty to say where they came from, since I reckon I don't rightly know."

Sebastien and Meghan watched as Colin flipped through the collection.

"That book there is yours for the rock bottom price of five dollars."

"Are you serious? Just five?" Colin was already reaching into his allowance money.

"Congratulations, young fellow," said Jasper, taking the cash.

The trio walked out of the tent and headed back into the festival crowd, making their way to the main road, where they were to meet up with Uncle Arnon and the Jendayas. They got to the road with just seconds to spare as Sebastien's father, Milo, pulled up his car.

Colin bounded to the rolled down window and showed them his new acquisition. After the youngsters piled into the back seat, the group headed to a small café, which resided in an out of use lighthouse at the end of the lake. Desserts were their specialty, in particular, the Whoopee Pie. Today's flavor: maple molasses, which included a layer of maple cream in between two round, chocolaty molasses cakes.

The group headed back to the central part of town to see what band was playing, and after a few more hours, Uncle Arnon decided it was time to head back home, as they were walking and he wanted to get home before dark. The Jendayas were staying in town to meet up with some local friends.

By the time the twins neared the camp, the sun was beginning to fade. They lagged behind, mostly due to the fact that Meghan's bootlace kept coming untied.

"Oh come off it!" she grimaced. "It never does this."

Up ahead, Uncle Arnon rounded the entrance into the campground.

"Don't be too long," he hollered back.

Meghan stopped again to tie her bootlace. Colin waited for her.

A branch snapped in the woods down the road a ways. Colin whirled around, searching cautiously. He saw nothing. They listened but all was quiet.

"Let's go," said Meghan. At the same moment, footsteps crunching on dead leaves echoed out of the woods. The twins hid behind a nearby tree trunk.

"Probably someone hiking through," thought Colin to his sister.

"Yeah probably," she thought back.

Still, they stayed hidden.

Down the dirt roadway, two shadows emerged from the pine thick and crossed the road, heading into the campground.

"Weren't they from the Gypsy camp?" asked Colin, thinking he recognized the two men.

"I think they are," agreed Meghan. *Wonder what they're up to?* Colin heard her thinking. "Let's get a little closer," she suggested in an excited whisper.

"Really? Closer? I don't think that is such a good idea, Sis."

She eyed him with her *we are doing it whether you want to or not* look.

"Fine," he conceded.

"C'mon," she encouraged. "We don't want to take too long." They did not take two steps, however, when two more people, this time definitely identifiable as men from the Gypsy camp, walked out of the woods.

Meghan grabbed Colin and they ducked into a ditch. This time, the two men stopped at the edge of the road and spoke to each other.

"All precautions have been checked and double checked, Vian Sadorus, sir. The schedule is set and we should be on time. Barring any unforeseen incidents, of course." He glanced into the sky, looking apprehensive.

"We are the last ones out, correct?" authoritatively questioned the one named Vian Sadorus. He was a fierce looking man that the twins recognized instantly, as he wore the same boisterous, too-warm-for-the-season coat.

"Yes, sir. We are the last out. Everyone else is back at camp, readying for departure."

The man named Sadorus nodded and the two crossed the road and disappeared through the woods toward their campsite.

"Why would anyone leave the camp through the woods?" asked Colin, bewildered.

Once the coast was clear, the twins dug themselves out of the ditch. As they wiped dead leaves and bugs off their clothes, Meghan eagerly stepped closer to the path the men had come from.

"There is no way they are leaving through there. They must have been talking about preparations to leave, while on a hike or something."

"I don't think so, Sis," Colin retorted. "No hiking gear. Couldn't have been going far, could they?"

"You know, that's true. Why don't we walk in a little ways? See what's in there."

"Uncle Arnon expects us home, we should get back," he reasoned, wishing he had kept his mouth shut.

"No weaseling. It will only take a sec. Like you said, it can't be far." She took off down the path.

Colin knew he would never live it down if he went back to camp without her. Tentatively, he followed. After just a few steps down the path, the pine trees were so thick that no sun could filter through. It was as if the sun had suddenly set.

"We better not get lost," said Colin, nervously.

"Shh. Use your inner voice, *just in case*." Meghan said through her mind.

"We better not get lost," he repeated with his inner voice. This time Meghan ignored him.

Fifty steps or so in they came to a small clearing where a fallen pine tree lay on the ground.

Surprisingly, most of the needles were still intact on the tree's long limbs.

"This cannot be where they were coming from," muttered Meghan, noticing fresh footsteps circling the tree.

"Inside voices please," shot Colin to her silently.

She scowled her reply.

"The path ends here, as well as the footprints," sent Colin.

The fallen tree had nine hidden spaces; each created by the way the pine branches had fallen. A few people could easily fit into each space at the same time.

"This would make an awesome fort," mused Colin, accidentally out loud. He corrected the mistake before Meghan could remind him about inside voice. "You could throw a lot of snowballs from this hideout," he added in his silent voice, while daydreaming of getting back at the camp bullies. Meghan did not let him linger in the daydream long.

"We better get back, Uncle Arnon's gonna worry if we don't get home soon."

Colin frowned. He had just started to climb through the tree. Meghan reached to seize his leg and pull him down, when overhead, they heard the distinct sound of heavy wings snapping against the air.

A tremendous shadow cloaked what small streams of light were trickling through the clearing.

The twins froze in position. Colin, clinging to a branch with one hand while sitting on one below, and Meghan, with her hand seizing his leg. Without moving, they tried to see what had landed.

"I've never heard wings that large before," sent Colin nervously. Something hovered over the tree. Something with red eyes that blazed brightly in the darkness.

Outside of their hidden tree room, a skidding thud brought them out of their frozen stupor. Whatever it was, it had landed!

"I knew this was a bad idea," Colin sent, with an, *I told you so* tone. Another pair of wings swooshed above, landing just a few feet away.

Colin squeaked. Meghan yanked on his pant leg motioning for him to shut up!

Whatever was outside the tree was walking the perimeter, repeating the twins' movements from a few minutes before; which meant before long it would find their secret room!

The shadow stopped and sniffed the air, like a dog.

It was close enough now that the twins could see directly into the piercing red and black eyes of the creature. Colin held his breath, afraid he would give away their hiding spot if he opened his mouth.

"Okay, I will *never*, not listen to you again," sent Meghan to her brother. Normally, Colin would have relished such a moment. Fear, however, gripped the occasion, as one of the creatures lunged to the top of a granite rock on the opposite side of the clearing.

"Where is the other one?" sent Colin. They searched frantically, without moving their bodies, but could not see it.

Finally, it joined the other, standing on the ground below the rock. From what the twins could see, the towering creature was hairless and gray skinned.

The wind picked up and the sky drew the two creatures' attention. The one on the ground lifted off, hovering just a few feet in the air. This gave Meghan and Colin a much better view of the body.

"What are they, Colin?" asked Meghan, stunned by what she was seeing.

"If I had to guess, I would say they are oversized... bats," he stammered silently, into his sister's mind.

"There are no bats that large!" she argued. "How is this possible? It's not!" she answered herself.

Colin gulped, not replying. The wind picked up even more, blowing leaves and branches off the ground, and violently shaking the fallen tree. Luckily, the needles held fast and did not fall off, keeping the twins' location to the intruders outside a secret.

The wind died quite suddenly, and with its end, someone else arrived; someone appearing to be human, but disguised in a dark cloak. The cloaked figure spoke, but the voice was deep and distorted, making it impossible to tell if it was a man or woman.

"Tonight, you will do what must be done," the figure spoke. "At midnight they will come. You will wait until the time is right, and then you will strike!" At the word strike, both creatures lifted up their wings, which measured at least ten feet across, and let out a ferocious snarl.

The creature on the rock sprung into the air, landing just a few feet from the twins. Their eyes popped open wide with disbelief and fear.

The face of the creature resembled a wolf, with long knife-like fangs. The wings looked like a flexible sort of webbing, with hook-like fingers that curled and clicked against each other, attached to thin, but muscular, arms that extended at least two feet beyond the web-like wings. The bottom half of the creature appeared more human than animal, with the exception of the toenails, which were long and jagged like rusted, broken, saw blades.

The twins reacted by leaning back into the depths of the tree, hoping to remain hidden.

"We need to get out of here," Colin managed to croak.

"How do you suggest we do that? There is no way we can outrun those things!"

Colin had no ideas and shifted on the branch. As he did so, his new book fell out of his sweater. Meghan caught it before it landed, but the book opened in her hand. The pages glimmered slightly, like bright dust settling.

"Did you see that?" she asked.

"Let me have it," he replied.

"You want to read it, right now? When we are this close to having our heads chewed off by whatever those things are?"

He grabbed it from her, making strange faces as he read. Meghan tried to tune in but his thoughts were incoherent.

"I need to get down from this branch," he sent her.

Meghan took the book, closed it, laying it gently on the soft ground, and then carefully and quietly helped her brother out of the tree and onto solid ground.

"Stay low, Sis. Less chance of catching that thing's eye," he said, sitting down, cross-legged. Meghan followed Colin, sinking to her knees. Her thoughts wandered. *We should have been home ages ago! I hope Uncle Arnon doesn't come looking for us.* Colin's heart raced, nearly bursting from his chest as he thought about their uncle happening unexpectedly upon these creatures.

Outside the tree, the voice spoke threateningly.

"Do not be seen, or heard, until the determined time!" The creatures were growling and clicking in a high-pitched screech, in what the twins could only assume meant agreement.

Colin sat on the ground with his new book, Magicante, but the strange shimmering that had been there moments ago had disappeared.

Another lofty breeze swept through the clearing setting off a chain reaction of events. First, this breeze sent the twins' scent to their unaware captors, and second, the pages of the book began to flip back and forth, the leaves on each page shimmering as if golden sunlight were beaming onto each leaf. Thirdly, the pages of the Magicante stopped flipping and to twins' surprise, words began forming on the leaf attached to the open page. It appeared in the form of fiery gold print.

"If you are capable of reading this, then you obviously need my help. You must ask for what you need."

"For what we need," repeated Colin.

Meghan shook her head, still disbelieving what she was seeing.

"Does it need to be specific?" Colin asked the book, trying to understand.

"Look!" pointed Meghan.

"Yes, of course specific. Since it appears you have no clue what you're doing, I suppose I will have to give you an example."

"Kinda rude isn't it," humpfed Meghan, realizing what she was saying. "This is ridiculous! This is some kind of stupid joke book, Colin. We need a real, safe and fast way outta here and back to camp."

A new message appeared on the leaf.

"That's the ticket! Knew you would get there eventually. So if you two are ready?"

Outside their hiding spot, the creatures were on the move, sniffing the air around the tree. The sniffing blended into growling and clicking noises, which the cloaked figure must have understood, as it swirled around, shouting angrily.

"Not alone?" the voice demanded. "FIND THEM! NOW!"

"I think we are about to have company," Colin spoke, his voice easily an octave higher than normal. In that same instant, a thought dawned on him. "Do you think these creatures are the ones scaring the Gypsies?"

"I somehow have a sneaking suspicion the answer is yes, but this is not the time, Col. We gotta get out a here!"

"I think the book is our only option," he said.

"What! Are you nuts?" asked Meghan. "You seriously think this book is going to just magically fly us away from here?" Meghan's fury was near equal to her fear of the creatures discovering their hiding spot.

"Maybe not, but do you see any other options?" Colin was not sure why he was defending the book. His gut told him to believe it. Ever since he could read, Colin had read book after book about magic. In fact, his uncle even encouraged his research on the subject, having given him numerous books on the topic himself.

The creatures methodically searched each open cavern in the fallen pine tree, edging closer and closer to where the twins were hiding.

"If this works," said Meghan, "I will never call you Little Bro again." She shook her head, her thoughts screaming, *I cannot believe I'm doing this!*

Colin wanted desperately to relish his sister's promise, but time was not on their side. The creatures were nearly upon them.

"On the count of three then," he sent to her. "We'll say together, take us to camp."

"And when it doesn't work?" she whispered. They held hands, with each of them grasping the book.

"Then, I guess..." he gulped deeply, his throat too dry to continue.

The creatures were at their room now, clicking and growling as their wolf-like faces started to poke inside. Smelling, and then seeing, the twins sitting on the ground set off a fury of howling and screeching. The cloaked figure ordered them to back away and strode toward them.

Here goes nothing! Colin thought to himself, unsure of whether anything would come out when he tried to speak. The twins jammed their eyes closed and counted.

"One... two... three ... TAKE US TO CAMP!"

They kept their eyes shut, fully expecting to be yanked from their hiding spot and hurled into the air, or mauled by the ferocious fangs of the hideous creatures outside.

All went quiet, neither twin breathed, and they kept their hands held together still gripping the book. The growls, clicking and screeching howls were gone. All the twins could hear was music; guitars playing somewhere not too far away. Meghan was the first to open her eyes. She did so slowly, and just one at a time.

"Holy crap!" she exhaled, hitting at her brother's arm.

He peeked through one eye, then the other.

They were sitting on the ground, a few feet into the woods behind the Jacoby travel trailer. The music they were hearing was from the Gypsy caravan.

"I am..." Meghan could not finish the thought.

"This is... " Colin shook his head, unable to think of a word strong enough to describe how he was feeling. He opened the book, stroking the pages with a fond new reverence.

To their further bewilderment, there was another message. However, this time the book spoke it.

"Those tremendous votes of confidence might well be enough for me to give up all of this *fun*, and retire," it said rather snidely. The twins sat in utter disbelief again, their eyes glued to the book.

"How... can... you... talk?" Meghan asked, as if she were talking to someone who spoke another language and could not understand her.

"I... will... not... answer... such... a... stupid... question!" the voice from the book retorted mockingly. It slammed itself shut, refusing to open again.

"Great, you've insulted it," said Colin.

"Listen to yourself! How can I possibly insult a book?"

"I don't know, Sis. But only *you* could."

"At least we are home," she said, standing up.

"Uncle Arnon!" Colin remembered urgently, shaking off the disbelief. They sped to the trailer, where to their relief he lounged on the front steps. He did not look happy, but at least he had not followed them.

"We took way too long. He looks totally miffed," said Meghan.

"Thanks a lot, now we're going to get grounded again." To their surprise however, Uncle Arnon did not get angry.

"That took you long enough. How many times did that boot come untied?"

"Sorry," they said in relieved unison.

Meghan added, "We got a little sidetracked. Saw a deer in the woods and decided to watch it for awhile."

It came out as more of a suggestion than an excuse.

"Deer eh? Just be careful. You never know what you might run into in these woods, not everything lurking out there is as friendly as a deer."

"Ain't that the truth," the twins mumbled together.

"What's that?" asked their uncle.

"Nothing," replied Meghan rapidly, for fear he might question them further.

"Man, I am spent!" Colin yawned, stretching. "I think I will head to bed early tonight."

Meghan followed him with a yawn of her own. Arnon gave them a curious look as they passed by, but did not argue.

"Night then," was all he said.

Once in their room they slammed the door shut and plopped down on the floor, sitting in complete silence.

"Tell me once more that it wasn't all just a bad dream," Meghan muttered after awhile. He did not tell her, but rather mustered up enough strength to lean forward and pinch her, hard, which followed by Meghan punching his arm.

"Nope. No dream," he winced.

"I still want to find out what those things were, and how they got here, and who they are planning on attacking later, and why!" said Meghan, with awakening vigor.

"And I really want to find Jasper Thorndike and ask him again where this book came from." After a pause he added, "Do you think we should tell Uncle Arnon?"

"Oh, no way, he would never believe it!"

"He believed in our telepathy," reminded Colin.

"This... This is way different, Colin."

He shook his head, in the end agreeing with her.

"Okay. I wanna pass something by you, Col. Maybe this is far fetched but..." she trailed off.

"What?" he asked eagerly.

"Remember, before we went into the woods and ran into those, bat-wolf things, who we saw coming out of that path?"

"Oh yeah, I'd almost forgotten, they were from... wait, do you think those things are here to attack Jae's caravan?"

Meghan shrugged, worried he would agree to her deduction. Colin considered the possibility.

"It is odd timing, that they are supposed to leave tonight, and they might be leaving via that path, and those screeches they keep running away from. It makes perfect sense, and *oh man*!" His heart sped up as he saw his sister's face.

"We need to warn them, Colin. Maybe we are wrong and they will think we are completely nuts. If we are right though, they might get hurt. Jae might get hurt, or maybe even killed."

"This is insane, Meghan! As much as I want to help Jae and his caravan, I do not want to go back out there in the dark, with those creatures nearby. It would be suicide," he whispered loudly.

93

"It won't be if we have the Magicante," she tried to convince.

"If you recall, the book sealed itself up. I couldn't get it back open." In attempts to prove his point, he tried once again to open the book, to no avail.

"Fine, Colin. You stay. But I am not going to sit back and do nothing."

He trembled, thinking of those creatures attacking Jae and his caravan without any warning.

"Okay," he agreed, defeated again. He added, matter-of-factly, "If we do this, how are we going to do it? I don't think we can simply walk up to their front door, knock, and say, hey, if you guys are thinking about any night time strolls through the woods to a certain fallen down pine tree, you may want to think twice. Because it just so happens that a couple of demented bat-wolf creatures want to attack you."

"That does sound a bit *too* crazy," agreed Meghan.

They paced back and forth, hearing Uncle Arnon go into his room and turn on his radio. It was getting late and the guitars at the camp were no longer playing.

Which meant only one thing: They were running out of time!

Chapter 4

The radio in Uncle Arnon's room was still on, giving the twins some cover as they continued pacing back and forth, racking their brains for an answer to their predicament.

"Can you see anything going on outside?" Colin asked Meghan.

"I don't see anything," she said, closing the curtain.

"Maybe we're too late. Maybe they have already gone," he said nervously.

"They couldn't have. We would have heard the caravans driving out. They have to pass right in front of our site."

"Meghan," Colin said slowly. "They walked in, remember?"

"Oh no, I had forgotten. We would still hear them, wouldn't we?"

"After what we saw in the woods, I am not sure I want to ask anymore questions like that."

"This is not helping. What are we going to do?" her frustrated voice said too loudly. They worried for a minute that their uncle would realize they were still up, but he stayed in his room, with no sign of movement.

A moment later Meghan was tearing up the carpet that covered the camper floor, revealing a secret trap door, one that their uncle had installed himself as an emergency escape. To this day, they had never needed to use it.

"Whoa," said Colin, quietly, but firmly. "What are you doing?"

"Going to find and warn them."

"No, no, no, I don't think so." He shook his head, for dual agreement.

"What, you chickening out?" she whispered angrily. "If they're already gone we have to find them, before it's too late!"

Meghan opened the trap door.

"Coming?" she asked, jumping to the ground cautiously. With her head sticking up into the trailer, she said, "It's not that I'm not scared, Colin, but I cannot let them walk into a trap, can you?"

"But we can't confirm that we're right," he protested, though his gut told him they were.

"Sometimes you have to take chances, *Little Bro*," she knew this would rile him.

"You promised," he whined.

Meghan sunk down below the floor hopeful that her brother would follow. Colin listened as she crawled along the ground and ran off into the darkness. He paced back and forth trying to gather the strength to follow.

"Okay, we really don't have any other choice," he finally concluded. Colin grabbed the Magicante and climbed down the escape hatch, closing it overhead. After a few steps, he slowed, waiting for his eyes to adjust to the dark, and searched for a glimpse of his sister. He called out for Meghan through his mind, but there was no answer.

"Great, she can't hear me," he thought. Caught off guard, Colin felt something seize his leg and pull him into the edge of the wood.

"Shhh. I think it's best to try and keep ourselves unseen."

"You could have just answered me," he scolded. His heart searched for its normal rhythm.

"Yeah, well, that's for taking so long to make up your mind."

Colin shook his head in disgusted aggravation.

"What exactly is your plan, Sis? We don't even have a flashlight."

"We can't have one," she said, sticking to the edge of the road. "We would be seen too easily. Besides, it's a full moon tonight. That should give us some light."

"You know, there are two full moons this month, which is why they are having the Blue Moon Festival. It only happens once every three years, or thereabouts."

"Good to see you've come back around. Can we stick to the task at hand, please?"

"Sorry, you know I can't help it when I get nervous," he replied.

They worked their way out of the campground, halting at the entrance leading to the fallen pine tree. They both searched the pathway for any sign of life, but all they saw was dark. Not even the light of the full moon could filter through. They looked up into the starry night sky; there was no sign of the bat-wolf creatures.

"You've got that book, right?" Meghan asked.

Colin secured the book under his arm.

"Got it. Whether it will work..." he trailed off.

"Let's go," commanded Meghan, stepping cautiously. Colin followed, sourness churning in his gut. The pathway was pitch black. The twins used their hands and feet to find their way through. After what seemed like an eternity, voices started filtering through the trees. Someone shouted orders.

"You guys, go over there, that door. Get lined up already. Not much time left. C'mon people, we need to be ready." It was the newly familiar voice of the man called Vian Sadorus, with the spiky hair and boisterous coat.

As they came into view of the fallen pine tree, observing from behind a leafy shrub, they were once again astonished. Small groups of Gypsies lined up at the entrances to the tree's secret rooms.

The man named Sadorus continued barking orders. It appeared that the group was almost ready for whatever was about to happen.

One woman, standing off to the right, immediately caught the twins' attention. She was tall and thin, almost gaunt; with hair of such a deep red, it looked nearly black. The full length, form-fitting jacket she wore swept across the ground, catching leaves as it shifted over them.

"I love that jacket," said Meghan, glancing at her own clothes. Colin listened to her thoughts; she was picturing the jacket on herself. *My hips are way too big to pull off that look.*

"Earth to Meghan," he beamed to her mind. "I cannot believe you are daydreaming about clothes."

"Oops," she shrugged.

"We need to find Jae," reminded Colin.

"Look," she pointed. "We're in luck. He's in the line closest to us."

"Now, how are we going to get his attention?" wondered Colin.

Out of the corner of his eye, Colin saw a foreboding silhouette fly overhead.

"It is time," the woman in the long jacket spoke, robustly.

She moved to the front of the fallen pine tree, with her back to the twins. "Once it opens, remember, you will have only five minutes until the door closes. Go safely! We will see each other on the other side."

Other side of what? asked the twins in simultaneous thoughts to each other. They pushed through the bush, almost into full view of the Gypsies.

"We are never going to be able to warn them," said Colin. "Without getting caught at least."

"Maybe we won't have to. Wherever they're going, they have to go fast apparently. What can happen in five minutes?" asked Meghan.

"We can still be stuck here," replied Colin, dryly.

"Not if Magicante works again we won't."

Colin started to open the book when bright light distracted him.

The fallen pine tree's rooms, including their hiding place from a short time ago, were filling with brilliant white light. The Gypsies began walking, and disappearing, into the brightly lit rooms.

Meghan and Colin realized that they had stepped into full view, as they had forced their way through the bush. They tried to back up but hit a branch, snapping it. They stopped, quite confident the Gypsies would notice them standing there. Only one of the smaller children noticed.

He appeared ready to give them away, but as luck would have it, pulled on Jae's arm and pointed at the twins. Jae squinted, trying to see what the boy was pointing at. A second later, someone picked up the little boy and carried him inside the pine room, vanishing.

Jae took a few steps closer and realized what he was looking at. He glanced around before dashing over.

"You should not be here," he told them. "There's no time to explain, you must leave!" His voice was pleading, not arrogant, or sad. Jae turned to go back.

An ear-piercing, shriek-mixed howl rang out of the sky, momentarily pausing the mass exodus. Seconds after, movement began again with renewed fervor.

The silhouettes of the fearsome bat-wolf creatures threw chilling shadows against the light emanating from the fallen tree. The woman in the red jacket shouted orders, with incredible calm.

"Everyone, get through now! Garner, assist me."

The man named Vian Sadorus rushed to her side as the creatures swooped down upon the Gypsies. Before they could land, or cause any harm, a blast of air hit the creatures, hurling them back into the night sky.

"What are they doing? Trying to fight those things?" asked Meghan, astounded anyone would attempt such a feat. They watched in stunned awe as the creatures reformed and attacked, while the woman and the man named Sadorus continued to fight, allowing the remaining Gypsies to flee.

The twins, if they did not leave soon, would be stuck alone, once all the Gypsies left. Reality thrust itself upon them when something flew in front of Meghan's face, bringing them out of their stupor.

She started jumping around, as if there were a spider crawling on her, shaking her clothes violently; in the process, she again moved out into the open. Colin rushed to her side and dragged her back.

"It was only a bird," he explained, sounding perplexed. He blocked from her that it greatly resembled the bird that had flown into her face a few days prior.

Another blast from the woman caught Meghan's eye.

"That woman's got style," she muttered, again mesmerized. Repeatedly, she and the man named Garner Sadorus blasted the beasts away. The twins took their eyes off the pair battling the creatures, to see that most of the Gypsies were gone and the light inside was beginning to fade.

"They must be safe once they're through," said Meghan, over the noise of the screeching and howling beasts.

"Meaning since we are still here, we are not," yelled Colin. "I think we should heed Jae's warning and get out of here, while we still can. They might be able to fight off those things, but we can't."

The only Gypsies remaining were the woman in her red jacket, Garner Sadorus, three others that were hastily hurling packages through, and Jae. He stood at the edge of a room, looking for the twins. A voice echoed for him to hurry. He paused, touching the entrance, but not stepping through. On the other side of the pine tree, all were now through. The light behind Jae was dimming fast.

The twins ran out from behind the bush, attempting to escape, but skidded to a stop when they saw Jae, still standing at the edge of the tree.

"The light is almost gone, Jae," yelled Meghan.

A distant voice begged Jae to hurry.

"Jae, GO!" demanded Meghan. "We'll be okay!" Overhead, the two creatures spotted the three youngsters standing below. They snarled and nose-dived toward them; one headed for Jae, and the other at the twins.

Jae bounded into the pine room as the creature swooped to where he had been standing, smashing into the ground.

The twins ducked and covered; the claws of the second diving creature missed them by inches. They lay on the ground watching it fly back up, preparing for another dive. The second creature bounded off the ground and joined it a moment later. Together, they hovered about twenty feet in the air and let out a howling screech more terrifying than anything the twins had ever heard before.

"Oh, crap!" cried Meghan. "Get out your book, Colin. We needed to leave like yesterday!" They crawled toward the tree room that Jae had just jumped into, which was now completely dark. As they moved closer to the entrance, a moan filtered out of the darkened pine tree. The twins froze, still on their stomachs.

"H - hello," stammered Meghan, hoping no one, or noth*ing*, would answer. A distressed face lifted up off the pine covered ground.

"Jae!" exclaimed Colin.

"Oh, no," said Meghan. They crawled inside and helped Jae sit up.

"What happened?" asked the twins.

"I waited too long," he answered slowly, trying to get his head about him. Hearing another shrieking howl was enough to bring them all back to reality.

Jae sprang to his feet.

"If we don't get out of here right now, we're dead! I cannot fight them on my own."

"We've got that one covered," said Meghan, adding under her breath, "I hope."

Colin had an idea.

"Book, um, Magicante, I'm sorry my sister insulted you, but we could really use your help right now."

It worked!

The book flung open and the cranky voice, only slightly audible over the screeching beasts, declared, "That took you long enough. Shall we go, then?"

"Hold hands," Colin yelled shakily.

Jae threw a distrustful look at the twins.

"What is that?" he demanded.

"Explain later," Colin said.

Meghan yelled for Jae to grab hold of the book. The shrieking was only a few feet away, and even through their pine cover, they could feel air swooshing under the creatures webbed wings.

"Uh, now, Colin," said Meghan, her eyes bearing down on him.

"Take the three of us to camp, NOW!" he shouted.

The shrieking and howling was instantly distant and once again, as they opened their eyes, they found themselves close by the Jacoby campsite, hearing only the distant howls of the creatures.

Jae's face appeared more stunned at the magical exit, than even by the twins' reactions to all they had seen that night.

"How did you do that?" he interrogated, backing away. "Who are you?"

"How did *we* do that? How about, who are you? And how do you do, what you do?" asked Meghan, thinking that her questions were much more important.

"Not that I don't want to discuss this," Colin snuck in, "But can we go somewhere more hidden?"

"We do need cover," agreed Jae, rather distrustfully. "I don't understand, though. How is it you know about magic?"

"Magic?" questioned Meghan.

"Some place safer, please," reminded Colin.

"Where Colin?" Meghan asked. "We can't just sneak Jae into the trailer. How would we explain it to Uncle Arnon?"

"He will understand, once we explain," said Colin, not believing a word he was saying.

"Uncle Arnon will never understand," Meghan said, agitated.

"But he wouldn't turn away someone in need of help."

"We would still have to explain that we went out after curfew," she reminded. The twins went on arguing, getting louder with each sentence.

"Hey!" Jae interrupted sharply. "You're going to wake up the whole stupid camp arguing so loud!" He took a deep breath, and added, "I think I have a solution, follow me."

The twins apprehensively followed Jae back to where the Gypsies had been camped.

"What are we doing here?" asked Colin, as the site was now empty. The wagons were gone.

"Just give me a second," said Jae with an air of impatience. "Apirire," he murmured, while waving his hand in front of him. Dusty air swirled in front of them, and when it dissipated a Gypsy wagon appeared.

"Where did that come from?" asked Colin, mystified.

"It was here all along, hidden," he answered dryly, opening the door. "We decided to hide them, seeing as it might be awhile before we returned."

It was the twins' first time being close enough to see the fine detail in the ornate woodcarvings that covered the outside of the wagon. They were surprised to see shapes of the bat-wolf creatures carved overhead.

The twins' thoughts swirled in their heads, feeling heavy.

"I promise we will be safe in here," insisted Jae, less arrogantly. He motioned for them to enter.

"What do you think?" Meghan asked her brother, silently.

"*Now* you care about what I think," he shot back. "We've come this far, we might as well see what's inside."

"Why aren't you going in then?" she asked.

He may have wanted to go in, but she knew he did not want to go in first.

"Ah, hello you two, up here," said Jae, impatiently. Meghan pushed Colin in front of her; his glare was piercing as he walked up the stairs. Meghan followed behind. Before entering, Meghan glanced sideways at Uncle Arnon's trailer; thankfully, there was no sign of movement.

As Colin stepped through the door, Meghan sensed his glare turn to awe and she understood why, once inside.

From inside, it did not look like a normal sized wagon at all, but rather a large banquet hall, equipped with a long wooden table, chairs, dishes and kitchen.

The main room was spacious, with the table taking up a good portion of the room. A cold, unlit stone fireplace covered half of the wall behind the table, while candle-filled wall sconces and chandeliers lit up the interior of the wagon.

"The candles are forever burning candles," said Jae. He held one in his hand to show them. "See, never burn down, will last forever."

Meghan wanted to ask how, but decided against it. They walked deeper into the room.

"It all makes sense now," said Colin. "This is how you fit all those people into just one wagon."

"You noticed that?" Jae said, surprised at Colin's keen eye. "Come on, I'll show you where my family and I lived while we were here." The twins followed him to a back wall, lined with doors. There was a copper knocker on the door, spelling the name Mochrie.

"Is that your family name, Mochrie?" asked Colin.

Jae nodded yes.

Inside was another room, much smaller. It included a velvet couch and chair set in front of a fireplace, also of stone. A teapot sat on the hearth next to a small pile of wood.

Jae continued the tour, although it was a quick tour, as the room contained just one corner desk and an old rocking chair. Four more doors lined the back wall of the room.

"Those are our bedrooms. My sister," he started tensely. "My sister and I share a room, and then my parents would be over there," he said pointing to another. He did not explain the two others doors.

The twins had many questions, and yet, no idea where to begin. Jae leaned over to the fireplace and waved his hand over the half-burnt wood inside; a roaring fire instantly warmed the room.

"Sit," insisted Jae to the twins, helping himself to the chair near the fireplace. Glad to get off their feet, they obliged and sat on the couch, across from him.

A few long minutes passed without any of the three speaking. Meghan and Colin were eager to ask questions, but Jae appeared deep in thought, leaning his elbow on the side of his chair, leaning his chin on his elbow. Meghan finally decided they had waited long enough.

"So, Jae," she startled him.

"Sorry," he said. "Got lost for a minute."

"How is all this possible?" asked Meghan. "I have never seen anything like this before."

Jae's eyes rose in suspicion and he motioned toward Colin's book.

"Appears you have seen a few things like it before," a bit of arrogance returned in his voice.

"I bought this book today," Colin explained. "I have no idea what it is, or where it came from."

"Today?" Jae questioned Colin, with a hint of disbelief. "Can I have a look?"

Colin, at first hesitant, handed over the Magicante, hoping Jae could shed some light on his recent purchase.

Jae flipped through the pages. "This is not familiar to me. Where did you get it?"

"From the flea market in town, at the Blue Moon Festival."

Jae closed it and handed the Magicante back to Colin.

"How did the book get us back here?" Jae asked.

"Honestly, I have no idea," shrugged Colin. "I believe it only happened because we were in danger and needed to get out of a place fast. There was a message on one of the leaves."

"There was a message on a leaf for you?" asked Jae.

Colin nodded yes.

"That is odd," said Jae, peering again at the book with great interest. Colin held the book closer, afraid for a moment he might want it again.

Jae laughed smugly.

"Don't worry. I have no need of that book, although, it did help us out of quite a jam."

"So that is our short and sweet story, how about yours?" grilled Meghan.

Jae took a deep breath and started.

"First, you have to understand that for the safety of my people, there is a lot I cannot tell you, and for your own safety, there are some things you cannot know." Jae's severe tone caught Meghan and Colin off guard.

"Can you at least tell us who you are, and what those horrific creatures are?"

"Those creatures, they are called Scratchers. And I hope after I leave, they will not decide to come back."

Colin interrupted. "You mean they might come back, later?"

"Yes, maybe no. The Scratchers hunt and kill my people. Sometimes we do not see them for months, and then sometimes, far too often."

"Those things are hunting you all the time?" reiterated Colin.

"Yes," Jae answered.

Meghan and Colin linked their minds to discuss this news without talking aloud to Jae.

"Do you think we should tell him about what we saw earlier tonight, Col? It *was* the reason we were trying to find them after all?"

"Maybe it could help them," Colin thought back. "If those things are hunting them all the time, it sounds like they need all the help they can get!"

"Jae, we have something to tell you," started Meghan nervously. "Maybe this will help, or maybe we were just really, really stupid and should not have followed you."

Jae leaned forward, intrigued by what they had to say.

"The reason we were there tonight was that we were trying to warn you. We followed a couple of your... people, into the woods earlier in the evening, yeah-yeah, bad idea," she agreed, seeing a look of *are you crazy* on his face. "Besides that point," she continued. "We ended up at the tree and those Scratchers arrived. We hid... in the tree."

"They were there, hours before?" cried out Jae in disbelief.

"Yes," answered Colin.

"How could they have known where we were heading?" Jae pondered over this question, gravely.

"Anyway," said Meghan, continuing. "We were stuck in the tree, confused as heck, and then someone else arrived. It looked like a person, but it was impossible to see for sure since their voice was distorted and they hid under a dark cloak."

"It's true then! There is a Scratchman," Jae said angrily, but not explaining further. He stood up and began pacing. "This is so unbelievable."

"Why do they hunt you?" asked Colin, boldly.

"Why? Many reasons I guess." It was clear he did not want to discuss why. "The most confusing part is that somehow, they always know where we are and where we are headed."

Jae looked at the twins, cautiously.

"How do I explain so it makes sense? You see, when I met you and said we travel a lot, this is true. What I left out is that we rarely travel here, in this reality, even though this is the world we are originally from."

The twins looked perplexed.

"We travel through doorways to other realities," he continued. "You might think of them as other realms or dimensions. The thing is, these doorways are said to be secure and closed, before and after we use them. It is a mystery as to how the Scratchers always track us down. Sometimes, like today, there will be just two. But other times there are more, many more."

"You mean there are more of them?" Colin's voice dropped and he sank into the sofa.

"Oh, yes. A lot more."

"Wait! Hold up a sec! I am still trying to understand this world travel thingy," said Meghan.

Jae explained again.

"There are doorways to other worlds, other realms, dimensions, realities... whatever you want to call it. You simply need the right key to open the door."

"I believe it!" exclaimed Colin. "It is just like all the books I read."

"It is all very real," said Jae, morosely. "We travel between worlds to survive. Always trying to stay ahead of the hunters, but never seeming to be able to do so."

"Can't you just hunt and kill them, instead?" asked Meghan, still perplexed.

"We tried. So far, though, we have not found a way to kill them, only to injure, temporarily."

"So if I get this all straight," sighed Meghan, trying to make sense of everything she had witnessed and heard that night. "You are Gypsies, with real magical powers, that travel between worlds, realities or whatever you want to call them, trying to escape those Scratchers, who hunt you, constantly, but you cannot kill them, or outrun them for long?"

"That about sums up what I can tell you safely," said Jae.

"And somehow, Colin purchased a book that also turns out to be magical in some way, and on the very day we would need it the most," she added.

"That mystifies me just as much as it does you two," noted Jae. "As I said, I have never seen a book like that before."

Silence overtook the threesome again and for a long time the only sound was the crackling of the fire. Jae was the first to break the silence.

"Even though it went awry, thanks for trying to warn us. I think what you have told me might be useful, if I can get back to my caravan."

"Can you rejoin them then? Do you know which world they moved on to?" asked Colin.

"Yes, I can get back to them. But not until the end of the month, you see, the door only opens at certain times and as you have seen, it does not stay open long."

Colin lost himself in thought for a moment.

"The blue moon," he blurted out. "It opens again on the second full moon, doesn't it?"

Jae grinned in impressed surprise. "Good guess."

"My brother watches a lot of Sci-Fi Channel," Meghan said, as an excuse for her brother's geeky brain.

"I've heard of that, never seen it though," Jae said.

Colin could have easily gotten them off subject discussing his favorite shows, followed by movies, and then books, so Meghan kept hold of the conversation.

"So basically, this means you have to stay here by yourself for an entire month. I am sorry, Jae. It is completely our fault. We thought you were in trouble."

"It can't be helped now, besides, maybe the information you gave me will help us better our fight. Still, I have never been away from my family before. We train for these situations, but it is the first time someone has not made it through in time."

Colin decided it was time to get back to the twins' original question.

"How do you do all this?" he asked, waving his arm and pointing to the inside of the wagon. "And who are you?" Jae sat quietly, as if struggling with an answer.

"The best way I can answer is to take you back to the beginning. When this world began, ages and ages ago, it was a magical world. Everyone knew of and practiced magic. The short version of the story is that there was a war; one that lasted many years. You could probably guess over what."

"Power?" assumed Colin. "It's the reason for nearly any war."

"And this war was no different. By the end of it, nearly every living person had been stripped of their magical powers. There were survivors though, and they banded together, hoping to better their chances of fixing what had gone wrong.

"Over time though, people forgot about magic and when it showed itself, they started to fear it. The survivors became outcasts, travelers trying to stay hidden from a world that no longer accepted them. They became the Svoda Gypsies, my ancestors."

"Wow!" said Meghan. "This is... a lot to take in."

"It's a lot even for me," added Colin. "I have always hoped real magic existed, but never dreamt it actually did."

"Welcome to the real world," Jae sighed. "It is not a pretty one, but yes, it is very much real."

"Oh crap!" Meghan suddenly let out. "Colin, do you realize what time it is?"

"You don't think Uncle Arnon is up yet, do you?"

"No, but we had better not take any chances. If he wakes up and finds out we are not in bed..."

"We are grounded for the rest of our lives!" Colin finished, already getting up to depart.

"Look. It is kind of our fault that you are stuck here, Jae. Whatever you need, we will do our best to help, until the second moon," insisted Meghan.

"Absolutely!" added Colin in agreement. "Will you be safe here, in the wagon alone?"

"I am fine here. Once you two leave, I will make the wagon vanish again. No one from the camp will even know I am still here. It's just one month. As long as the Scratchers stay away, I'm golden!" he smiled, wistfully.

"We will come back and check on you tomorrow then," advised Meghan, as they departed the wagon. Colin waved goodbye and as they stepped onto the ground, the wagon dissolved into nothing, vanishing before their weary eyes.

The twins tiptoed their way home. Thankfully, Uncle Arnon's snoring told them he had not awakened during their absence. They covered up the secret escape hatch on the floor. Colin put the Magicante on the bookshelf and the twins climbed into bed. Both were exhausted, and yet found they could not sleep.

Giving up, Colin sat up, leaning on his elbows. "Sis," he sent wearily, sensing she was also still awake.

"Yeah, Col."

"If I had to wager, I would bet that these last few days did not actually happen."

"I thought we had already figured that out, when you pinched me and I punched you, and we were both wide awake."

"I know, I know, but magic. I can't believe it's real. Even crazier though is that I got this book today," he said, stroking the cover as it sat on the shelf. "Maybe I was meant to buy it, so we could help Jae?"

"I am not sure we helped anything. We got him stuck here," argued Meghan.

"Jae didn't seem overly concerned. His family must be though." As the twins lay back down, sleep finally came. Visions of dark shadows and bright lights filled their dreams.

Colin awoke three different times, believing for sure that he had heard Scratchers in the distance. Meghan reassured him that this time, she thought for certain it *was* just an owl, and begged him to go back to sleep. After the third time she yelled into his mind, "We have to get up soon enough as it is, Col, go back to sleep already!"

'Soon enough' did come too early for the twins. In the blink of an eye, the smell of brewing coffee infiltrated the trailer. The twins, as tired as they may have been, were eager to see Jae.

"How are we going to work out the Sebastien factor?" asked Colin. "Can we tell him? I hate the idea of lying to him."

Meghan had not thought about Sebastien. So much had occurred since they had seen him the evening before.

"I guess we will have to feel it out, plus, I don't think it's our decision to make, its Jae's."

"I suppose you're right. We should come up with a story as to why Jae is here. Adults are bound to be suspicious…"

"And ask questions," Meghan finished his thought. "And he cannot stay hidden in the wagon for the entire month." She then looked directly at Colin with her warning face.

"You better not blow this, Colin! Make something up! Lie! We cannot tell Uncle Arnon or Sebastien, at least not for now."

"Why do you always think I will be the one to ruin everything?" he spat back.

"Because, Colin Jacoby, you have never successfully told a lie in your entire life! You always give yourself away."

"I can't help it. I'm not a professional liar like you!"

Meghan gasped, and sighed. Yes, she told a few fibs here and there, but it had saved her hide along with Colin's on numerous occasions. She hid her thoughts from him, embarrassed that she felt mortified by what he had said. *I only lie when I have no other choice. Don't I?*

Meghan decided to ignore him and sauntered into the kitchen to make breakfast. They hurried to eat and get dressed. Colin even helped Meghan clean up, without her ordering him to. Once they were ready to leave the trailer, their uncle, while still sitting at the kitchen table reading the newspaper, said, without even moving his eyes from what he was reading, "Hope you two had a good time last night. You realize you're both grounded, right?"

Chapter 5

To the twins' bewilderment, Uncle Arnon did not question where they had been the previous night. He did however, find ways to keep them annoyingly busy over the next few days, and did not allow them out of his sight. They desperately wanted to visit Jae and whenever they could, stole glances next door, in hopes he would give them a sign, indicating he was still safe.

Colin mentioned nervously, at least ten times during their punishment, that at least there had been no sign of the Scratchers.

Sebastien visited daily, under strict guidelines. They had to be either in the trailer or within sight of the trailer, and always, within Uncle Arnon's view.

When Sebastien found out that the twins had been grounded, he was at first hurt, as they had gone on some crazy adventure without him. Meghan was quick to point out that then he, too, would be in trouble if he'd joined them. This smoothed things over, for now. He did try, repeatedly, to get the twins to explain what they had snuck out to do.

Their luck held though, and they never found the need to come up with a false story, as their uncle continually had himself within earshot. Sebastien knew they would not talk about it in front of him.

During the evening on the fourth day of their torturous punishment, Sebastien arrived, toting goody bags full of sugary treats. He emptied it out on the kitchen table and all their faces hungrily drooled over the pile. There were whoopee pies, crème horns, devil dogs, maple sugar candy, bismarks, and three different kinds of fudge.

After gorging themselves into sickness, Uncle Arnon, chuckling lightly, announced they were no longer grounded. Meghan and Colin assumed that their sickly faces, green from the over abundance of junk food, combined with all the work he had made them do, was finally sufficient.

It could also have had to do with the fact that someone needed Uncle Arnon, the handyman, on the other side of the camp, or that he was just sick of being stuck at the trailer watching the grounded twins.

Regardless, in just minutes, the twins could finally check on Jae Mochrie.

"Only one problem," sent Colin to his sister.

"I can't ask Sebastien to leave. Maybe one of us could go and the other stay here?"

"Okay, but which of us does what? And how will the other make an excuse to leave?" They did not mind allowing this problem to stew for a while longer, being that their sugar-filled, rumbling bellies greatly discouraged them from moving.

Sebastien solved their dilemma by stretching and yawning, over-dramatically.

"I think I'll go now. Maybe hit the hay early tonight. Now that you're not grounded anymore, we can hang tomorrow."

"Are you sure?" Meghan questioned their easy luck. Colin wondered if Sebastien had somehow read their minds. Meghan caught onto his thought.

"NOT!" she yelled back silently, aghast at the thought. Aloud, she said, "It's still early Sebastien."

"Are you nuts, we want him to leave, don't we?" shouted Colin in her head.

"That does not mean we should act like it," she said. Sebastien's eyes darted between them, realizing they had been speaking without him being able to hear, again.

"Why don't you guys tell me what is going on?" interrogated Sebastien. He stood with his arms folded, waiting.

"Say something," urged Colin.

"Why me? What should I say? Can I just tell him?"

Sebastien shook his head and left the trailer.

"Wait," shouted Meghan, running after him.

"I realize that being grounded and stuck in the trailer, you couldn't tell me what's going on," Sebastien said. "However, your uncle is gone, and you still don't want to tell me. And then you sit there and have your private conversations with each other, forgetting that I'm even here!" He turned to leave but Meghan grasped his arm, stopping him.

"Wait a second!" she pleaded. She had never seen Sebastien so angry. He stopped, waiting for her to speak. Meghan stumbled for the right thing to say.

"I. Well. I mean. We are not talking about you. You understand that, right?"

"I didn't actually think you were," he said dryly. "But that's not the point."

"What is the point, then?" asked Colin.

"The point is, you are always doing it, even when you think no one is paying attention. You leave everyone out of your conversations."

The twins finally realized that he felt left out.

"What if we promise to try really hard not to do it?" squeaked Meghan. Sebastien was their oldest friend; they certainly did not want to jeopardize that.

"Usually, it's not so bad. This summer though, seems you two have a lot going on up there."

The twins were stuck. Did they admit Jae's story to keep their friend? Their only alternative was to lie, and hope he forgave them if he found out.

"Lying is starting to get too complicated," Meghan quickly sent to Colin. Maybe we should just tell him?" She did her best to pretend she was paying attention to Sebastien as she said it.

"I don't see how we are going to get through the next month without telling him," Colin shot back.

Meghan took lead.

"Sebastien, there *is* a good explanation. If you would," she paused, her eyes grazing Jae's hidden camp. "I think the best way to explain is to follow us."

Colin cringed with uncertainty. What if Jae was not home, or did not answer. Sebastien would think they had gone mad. Moreover, they were just as unsure about how upset Jae would be, since they had not visited, after promising to help him.

Instead of going out to the road, they made their way through the trees separating the two camps.

"Where are we going?" asked Sebastien.

"You'll see," answered Meghan, as they came into the deserted looking site. "It's around here, somewhere." Meghan felt the air for the wagon. Colin followed her lead.

"Have you gone crazy? There's nothing here," Sebastien grimaced.

"It's very close, I think."

Why could they not find it? Had Jae moved? Worse, had he left and not told them?

"What do we do now?" asked Meghan.

"Maybe he can hear us, if we yell."

"I don't think we can look any crazier," she mumbled.

"Jae, where are you?" they called out in unison.

Sebastien took a few steps back, not wanting to be so close to two people yelling into nothing.

"Why are you guys yelling for Jae? The camp is empty. They all pulled out a few nights ago."

The twins did not answer. The Gypsy wagon, which was indeed right in front of them, materialized. The ornate wooden door flew open and Jae popped into the entrance, smiling.

"We hope this is all right, Jae," said Meghan, biting her lip and pointing to Sebastien. Who in turn gaped at the wagon and Jae. He tried to speak, but nothing came out. Meghan pulled him up the stairs, coaxing him inside.

"I had a feeling I might see you again, Sebastien. Welcome to my home away from home," said Jae, alleviating the twins' worries.

Sebastien walked in with the same awe on his face that the twins had shown when they first entered the wagon.

Colin explained their absence, anxious that Jae might be angry they had not visited.

"We got caught for being out the other night. Uncle Arnon had us working our butts off! Sorry we couldn't get over here sooner."

"I guessed as much," said Jae. "I was watching you from my window. It was quite entertaining, actually, watching the two of you working."

"Glad we could be of assistance," said Meghan crossly. She turned to Sebastien, still stunned.

"I am not even sure where to start. Obviously, you remember, Jae."

"Yes, of course, how... are you?" Sebastien asked awkwardly.

The twins sat him down at the long table close to the stone fireplace and retold the tale of first, following the Gypsies into the woods and encountering the Sctratchers, then escaping via the aid of the Magicante. Throughout the retelling, all Sebastien mustered out were exclamations of, "No way" and "For real," to "I know I'm sitting here, but I don't believe it!"

They finished with explaining the reason they had snuck out and been grounded, and how Jae came to be accidentally left behind, unable to rejoin his caravan for nearly a month. Once their tale was complete, they allowed Sebastien the first word, once he was ready to speak.

"Okay, if I have this correct, magic is real, and Jae is stuck here and being hunted by some kind of flying monster that I hope never to encounter?"

"I think you're getting the picture," Meghan replied, patting him on the back.

"I am not stuck here permanently, though. When the second moon rises, the door can reopen. I would bet my life my dad will come for me," Jae said knowingly. Sebastien nodded that he understood, although his face said otherwise.

"*Our job* is to make sure he gets there on time, and in one piece," said Colin.

Jae showed Sebastien around the rest of the wagon and even though the twins had seen it before, it was still captivating. They made themselves comfortable around the fireplace in Jae's room.

"Are you managing okay over here?" asked Colin.

"To be honest, I am bored out of my mind. Definitely ready for an excursion outside the wagon."

"Is it safe for you to leave the wagon, with the Scratchers still out there?" asked Meghan.

"I do not think we will see them until it is time for the door to reopen, but if they do show up, I am rested and ready to fight!" he said with vigor.

"We need a story then," suggested Sebastien. "A reason that you are at the camp, without parents being around."

"Colin and I tried to come up with one over the last few days, but we got nothing!" Meghan told them.

"Every time we thought we had a story that would work there were always holes. Like someone is bound to recognize you as being from the caravan," Colin added.

"I think I have the perfect solution then," announced Jae. "Its something I have been working on over the last few days, in between watching you guys working," he laughed. Meghan, Colin and Sebastien listened intently to Jae's idea.

"You see, I know a magical spell that can alter my appearance. Not a lot, but maybe just enough to make anyone question that they recognize me."

"You can do that?" Meghan, Colin, and Sebastien asked all in unison.

"Yes," he answered smugly. "At least I can now," he clarified. "It is kind of hard to explain. You see, it takes a lot of magical energy to keep up any sort of spell, and even more for a transformation spell, but during the last few days of being alone, my energy is surging. I have never felt so strong. Like I could pull off any spell I wanted to!" His eyes filled with excitement.

"Let's see it then," demanded Meghan. "If this works, none of us will be stuck inside anymore!"

Colin and Sebastien nodded their agreement.

Jae clapped his hands and winked.

"Watch this," he said. He turned his face away from his audience and waved his hand, saying something they could not understand. When Jae turned back around his hair was no longer long, dark and stringy, but shorter, auburn and spiky. His eyes changed from brown to green, and a few freckles ran over his pale-skinned face.

"Wow! Magic can never get old in my book," said Colin. The others agreed, amazed at the change.

"My dad would be so angry if he saw me doing this," Jae admitted. "I've been practicing all kinds of looks he'd never approve of."

The twins and Sebastien laughed as Jae spent the next thirty minutes trying out different styles and colors, until finally settling on the original, auburn spiky hair.

"It is definitely different enough that no one would be able to place you, Jae," insisted Meghan, wishing she could change her appearance as easily.

"I think I have come up with a good story as to why your parents are not around," Sebastien told the group. "We can say your parents work in town during the day, and if you are with us at night, they have been working hard all day and have already crashed for the night."

The three waited for Jae to make the call.

"I think it's just brilliant enough to work!"

Sebastien shook his head as the foursome departed the wagon.

"This is a lot to take in," he admitted.

"You had better hope you don't have an encounter with those Scratchers," said Colin. "They will make an instant believer out of anyone."

"That is certainly the truth!" agreed Jae. "Let's not think about it now, though."

"You're right!" yelled Meghan, spinning around in circles. "We are all free. Let's have some fun!" She took off running. The others laughed and followed.

Later that night, as the twins crawled into bed, Uncle Arnon walked in their room.

"Your big thirteen is practically here," he sighed. "I hate to be so blatant, but are there any particular gifts that you have in mind? I am plum out of ideas."

The twins laughed, as this happened each year.

"At least you know you are a terrible shopper," joked Meghan.

"Terrible indeed!" he agreed.

"Besides, you already bought me my gift," reminded Meghan, tapping her nose.

"This is a special year, though," Arnon said. "You only turn thirteen once."

The twins connected their minds.

"I think we should answer the same as we always do," said Colin.

"Yeah. I know he doesn't have a lot of extra money to spend, thirteenth birthday or not," Meghan said, somewhat dreamily. Colin caught on to her thoughts on wearing clothes that were actually black, not faded black. Their thoughts then disconnected.

"I will leave it up to you, Uncle Arnon," Colin said. "There really isn't anything in particular I would like." Meghan nodded her head in agreement. Arnon eyed them suspiciously.

Being paid for handyman jobs in trinkets, casseroles and cobblers made it hard to afford the daily essentials, never mind splurges like birthday parties.

"I think I am mostly happy that once we hit the big one-three, we get the extra hour on curfew," added Colin.

Arnon patted his shoulder.

"Could I ask for more in two youngsters?" he muttered. "Goodnight, you two. Sleep tight." He left the room, closing the door behind him.

Mere minutes later the twins were out cold. Having not been able to visit with Jae over the last few days had interrupted their sleep in the previous nights.

The days leading up to their birthday party were much the same; lounging by the lake, wandering around the campground or into town, and overfilling themselves on ice cream and whoopee pies. Uncle Arnon met Jae with great success. He was thrilled they had another friend to invite to the birthday party.

The day before the big birthday, Sebastien told the twins he had to go into town with his parents. Jae decided to tag along. The twins had a sneaking suspicion they were shopping for birthday gifts. Uncle Arnon was out making a last minute camp call; someone's shower had gone berserk. They also had a feeling this was a ploy, after they caught him arm in arm with Kanda Macawi, hightailing it out of the campground. They fully suspected that he had joined up with Jae, Sebastien, and his parents, in birthday shopping.

Colin, eager to learn more about his new book, leaned against a granite rock near the trailer and flipped through the pages of the Magicante.

As the hours passed, Meghan, bored, lazily turned the pages of a magazine, looking at new hairstyles and clothes. *Speaking of clothes, this sweater is killing me.* She took it off, feeling overheated.

"You feeling okay?" Colin asked, seeing her wipe sweat from her forehead.

"Fine. Just a little hot out here."

Colin did not think it was hot at all.

Meghan's thoughts strayed to how cool it would be if she could change her appearance, like Jae. She wondered what she would change if she had the choice. She had always thought about cutting her hair shorter, but had never dared. She grimaced at her chest, thinking, something there would be nice, too.

"Eeeeewww," shouted Colin. "I didn't need to hear that!"

Meghan's temper grew fiery at once.

"Then why were you listening?" she slammed down her magazine. "You shouldn't butt in if you don't want to hear!" She knew she'd let her guard down, and would have done the same to him. She stomped off angrily, storming down the camp road, too easily allowing her fury to escape.

Colin threw the book down, leaning back. *Her temper gets worse by the day!* He forgot to block the thought and felt his sister's mind go blank as she put up her own block, but not before hearing her scream profanities, meant for him.

The sun popped out from behind a cloud, pouring comforting rays of heat across his face. His eyes closed and he started to doze, forgetting about his sister. A short while later, cloud cover blocked the sun, stealing his sleeping potion. A strong breeze made him shiver and he opened his eyes. The breeze continued to pick up.

Colin jumped up, alarmed, when his book flew up into the air and then fell, landing with a thud. It opened itself and the pages began to flip back and forth. The leaves began to shimmer and glow, detaching themselves from the pages. They formed a whirling tornado, which sped down the camp road.

The cranky voice of the Magicante spoke, with concerned sternness.

"Find your sister, Colin, and do so with haste! She cannot face what is coming alone!"

"What do you mean?" he yelled at the book, his heart pumping heavily. "How am I supposed to find her, she's blocking me. I don't know where she went!"

The book said nothing else and slammed shut.

Colin grabbed it off the ground and ran after the tornado, hoping it would lead to Meghan.

"I hope it's not the Scratchers!" he thought to himself. He listened, but the skies were quiet. "I'm sure I would hear them. But what else could be happening?"

His panic heightened as he followed the tornado, which veered off into the woods.

Surprisingly, it destroyed nothing in its path; plants and trees miraculously bent out of the tornado's way, allowing Colin to pass through, before standing erect once again.

He opened up his mind, searching for Meghan. At first, he could only sense that she was close by, and then like a flooding river her thoughts poured into his mind. It was a mixture of panic, fear and confusion. She was fighting something, but he could not make out what.

"If its Scratchers, we are so screwed!" he shouted to no one. "I cannot fight those things."

His short legs darted easily through the pathway cleared by the leaf tornado. He could sense that she was somewhere just ahead. Then, a clear picture entered his head of Meghan, doubled over in pain, kneeling underneath a twisted oak tree.

"Meghan! Hold on I'm coming!" he yelled, hoping she could hear him. The pain she was feeling intensified and Colin nearly fell over as the same feeling filled his own mind. He blocked her for fear that he would not be able to continue standing if he did not.

Seconds later, he skidded to a stop and dropped the Magicante onto the ground. The twisted oak towered in front of him. The pages of the book began flipping back and forth as the leaves once again affixed themselves back to their pages.

Colin found Meghan on the ground beneath the oak.

"Get it off me!" she screamed. "Get it off!" her arms flailed as if she were trying to bat away a horde of stinging insects. Colin leaned down and tried to pick her up, only to instantly let go when she shrieked in anguish.

"Tell me what's wrong," he begged her. However, the only reply was another horrifying scream, followed by incoherent thoughts in which Colin believed he heard the words 'please let me die.'

Fire consumed Meghan's surroundings. Orange and crimson flames burnt the trees, the ground, the sky, and an approaching figure. She gasped, horrified as the flames edged closer to her own body. She tried to move but was frozen, unable to get away from the approaching fire.

Meghan screamed as the first of the flames touched her skin. This time, unlike her nightmare, she felt the fire burn her. She tried to push her body away from the flames, but still could not move.

"Get it off me!" she yelled. "Get it off!"

The flames licked at her legs, spreading to her arms, and then to her head. The heat burned at her throat cutting off her air and she gasped for breath. She wished desperately to pass out, or even to die.

"Why haven't I died?" she wondered. "It cannot take this long to burn to death!"

Meghan left the thought behind as a new wave of pain overwhelmed her. The burning figure had touched her. Each touch of the figure's hands left the sensation of a sharp knife cutting into her already burning skin.

She let herself fall to the ground, wishing for it to end, even if that meant death.

Colin, desperate for help, opened the Magicante, hoping it would take them home as before, but this time the voice had an unwelcome response.

"I am truly sorry boy, but you are on your own this time. You have another way."

Colin did not understand. What did the book mean by another way?

"Colin," mumbled Meghan.

"I'm right here. Hang on," he told her, furiously thinking of how he would get her home. In his haste, his hand brushed against her forehead.

"Ouch!" he yelled, yanking it away. Meghan's skin was a hot as a skillet. "She shouldn't even be alive," he said aloud. He had never heard of a fever like this before.

Colin pleaded with Magicante.

"I don't understand what you mean by another way."

"I am not without compassion, boy," replied the book. "But you have little time to prepare. You *must* do this on your own!"

Colin stared at his moaning sister, blocking her thoughts so he could think.

"What's my other way?" he asked himself. He had no idea what the Magicante wanted him to do.

Meghan wanted to sink into the fiery ground around her. Somehow, though, through the pain and fear, a strange thought popped into her mind. *Am I really on fire?* Flames had spread across her body, but underneath them, her skin was still there. There was no smell of burning flesh. The fire felt a though it were burning from the inside.

"Boiling blood," she whispered aloud in her delirium. She laughed hysterically.

Colin heard her and decided that one way or another, he had to get her home, fast! He took hold of Meghan, trying to lift her off the ground to see if she could stand. An agonizing scream tore at his eardrums and he let her sink back down to the ground, dropping her.

"She's dying," he thought, horrifically. "And I can't stop it!"

Meghan heard a muffled voice echoing snidely through the flames, and recognized it as the voice from the Magicante.

"You can stop the pain faster if you would just let Colin help you already!"

Realizing that the figure had to be Colin, she did not stop him when he attempted to come near her again. She was afraid, though, that she might burn him if he touched her. She focused all her remaining energy on seeking out his thoughts.

"Meghan, can you hear me," he kept repeating. "I do not want to hurt you, but I have to get you home, okay." She could not answer but managed to nod her head that she had heard him. She lost his thoughts and her own returned. The pain, if possible, intensified. She could not help but scream.

Colin held the now useless Magicante under one arm and grasped Meghan with the other. He closed his eyes tightly and wished desperately to understand what the book meant by another way. Meghan's breath started coming in gasps.

"I just want to go home!" he bellowed hopelessly.

As soon as he had said it, the ground began to whirl beneath him. He gasped, grasping Meghan tighter. She screamed louder. Her mind opened up and he could no longer block her thoughts from penetrating his mind. He was overwrought with pain and anguish and screamed along with her. For a brief moment, he could feel exactly what she could feel.

A moment later, they were inside their uncle's trailer. His thoughts of, "How the heck did I do that?" vanished instantly, replaced by the need to help his sister. He gently laid her on the couch, grabbing a glass of cold water. She knocked it from his hand when he tried to get her to drink it.

Familiar voices echoed in the distance. He sprinted out of the trailer in one long step, at the same time wailing, "Uncle Arnon!" The distress in his voice caused his uncle to drop the packages he carried, and dash toward Colin.

"What is it?" Arnon pleaded, taking hold of his shoulders.

"Meghan. She's having some kind of fit, and she's burning up."

Arnon ran to the trailer with Kay Jendaya's petite frame at his heals.

"You all stay here," she ordered as they disappeared inside.

Colin collapsed to the ground. He could not recall ever feeling this tired, or, more relieved to have a grown up around.

"Help him up, boys," instructed Milo. Sebastien and Jae took one arm each, and helped him stand.

"What happened?" asked Sebastien, his voice trembling.

"I have no idea." He did not wish to explain what had truly occurred, at least, not with Sebastien's father around.

"This might take awhile," said Milo. "Why don't we all go back to our camper, and I will make us something to eat." Milo tried to smile, but after the horrified look on Colin's face, the last thing any of them wanted was food. Colin wanted to go back into the trailer, but he let the others lead him the other way. On the walk to the Jendaya camp, they attempted to make themselves feel more confident about Meghan's condition.

"She probably just has a bad case of the flu," suggested Jae. "My aunt did once, had a real high fever and hallucinated like crazy, but she was fine after."

"She can't possibly be sick on your thirteenth birthdays," reminded Sebastien. "She has been waiting for this one forever. I bet you by tomorrow morning she's good as new."

Hours went by without a word. Evening became night, and Jae disappeared at one point, saying he needed to go home and let his parents know where he was. He returned about thirty minutes later, looking more worried than ever. It also put the boys in a situation they had hoped to avoid, a conversation with adults about Jae.

"So what do your parents do, Jae?" asked Milo a few minutes later.

"Teachers," he answered without hesitation. "They travel around helping students having difficulties, keeps'em real busy."

Colin and Sebastien took noticeably deeper breaths, and tried to get back to the topic of Meghan before Sebastien's father could question Jae further.

"Should we go and check on them, maybe they need help?" asked Colin, unsure of how much longer he could sit and wait for news of his sister. The others agreed, but Milo said he thought it best for them to wait, and continued monotonously stoking the fire.

As the night crept on, the chill of the air forced them closer to the fire. Sebastien excused himself after awhile, disappearing into the camper. Upon returning, he brought along some tonics. Colin noted that his face was ashen as he handed them out.

Finally, shortly after midnight, tired footsteps faintly headed in their direction; they each stood and breathlessly waited for a shadow to emerge from the darkness. It was Arnon. Colin was the first to bombard him, followed by the rest.

"How is she? What happened? Is she all right now?"

Arnon sat down, wearing exhaustion on his face. He raised his hand for them all to sit.

"She will be all right." Everyone sighed in relief. "But..." he continued, pausing as they inhaled, waiting with baited breath. "It may take some time."

They exhaled again.

"How long?" asked Colin.

"A week, maybe longer," he replied, adding, "We'll have to postpone the birthday party."

"Of course," Colin said expectantly.

Sebastien braved the next question.

"So what is wrong with her?"

"We had a local doctor come by. She picked up some kind of fever, but on the good side, it is not contagious in any way."

"Well that is something at least," said Milo.

"Kay is going to sleep with Meghan tonight. I hope that is okay."

"Yes, of course it is perfectly fine. We can all crash here tonight, give Meghan some space to recover," declared Sebastien's father. "Jae, you are welcome to stay if it suits you."

"Actually, I think I will go home and come back first thing tomorrow."

Colin and Sebastien escorted him to the dirt roadway.

"Are you sure you don't want to stay?" asked Sebastien. "There is plenty of room."

"I might be able to see if anything happens from my wagon. I will keep watch and report to you guys if I see anything."

Colin was jealous and at the same time, glad that Jae would do this.

"Is there anything... magical you could do for her?" he asked, not sounding hopeful.

"No, I am afraid I do not know much about healing, other than cuts and bruises. I am more apt to make it worse. When I disappeared earlier I did try to get a closer look, but I did not see much."

Both Colin and Sebastien watched as Jae evaporated into the night, to where his pretend parents were supposed to be camped, jealous that shortly, he would be closer to Meghan.

"He wouldn't actually try anything that would make her worse, would he?"

"No. I think he just feels bad for her," said Colin.

"If something does happen for the worse, he will come back faster than my mom or your uncle would," decided Sebastien.

They headed into the trailer and Colin crawled into the bottom bunk below Sebastien, but sleep would not come. His thoughts strayed to the magic that had somehow gotten them home. The book had probably helped in the end, he told himself. He could not have performed magic all on his own. It simply was not possible.

Meghan did not understand how she was not burning everything her body touched. The flames, which still licked every inch of her skin, did not burn anything, including her own body. Even though the pain was unbearable, this understanding somehow calmed her. She was in pain, but maybe if this ended she would not have any permanent damage done to her body. It was also a relief that she would not hurt anyone else.

A new wave of heat swept through her body, and although her thoughts were more clear, in the fact that she was not actually on fire, her body still felt as though she were burning alive. She let out a moan and started to panic when she lost her breath. Her body seized and she started thrashing so violently that she nearly fell off the sofa.

A tall figure came closer, followed by another. Cold, wet hands pressed on her face and for a moment, she could see the face of Kay Jendaya staring down at her. She heard desperate voices around her, whispering words she could not understand. Finally, Meghan could stand the pain no more and lost all strength, falling into unconsciousness.

The searing pain that penetrated her body dissolved into weightless content. She slept. Throughout her sleep, distant voices echoed frantically, but still, she could not understand them. Then, abruptly as it left, the pain came slicing back into her mind, tearing her from her peaceful slumber.

Meghan's body jolted upward. She took deep, painful breaths. Her eyes focused just long enough to see the face of a stranger kneeling beside her. This stranger placed her hand on Meghan's chest and gently pushed her back down onto her back.

She heard the strange woman speak things she could not understand and the pain disappeared again. This time, Meghan did not descend completely into unconsciousness. But exhaustion prohibited her from doing anything but keep still and listen to the voices surrounding her.

In the trailer, Uncle Arnon, Kay Jendaya and Kanda Macawi watched over Meghan. Minutes later, there was a faint knock at the door. Arnon nodded toward Kay and Kanda, knowing who it was.

"Ameila," he said opening the door. "Please come in." She entered and immediately took hold of his hand.

"Hello, Arnon. It is good to see you. Although, I wish it were under better circumstances."

"This situation is most unexpected," he said.

"Indeed," she answered, looking down at Meghan.

"She's a Firemancer," whispered Kanda Macawi. "I have never seen the change take place in such a violent manner."

"Is there nothing more we can do for her?" begged Arnon, his voice hollow.

"I have every person capable researching now," insisted Amelia. "I am so sorry, Arnon. As you said, this is a most unexpected turn of events."

"On the bright side, if there is one to this cruel torture," continued the woman named Amelia, "is that this just might be the clue we have been looking for all these years. As you know, we already have our theories as to their father's identity, which is why they have been in hiding. However, Firemancy is not a common gift and always stays within family bloodlines. We are closer than ever to discovering who the twins' mother really is."

"Have you considered that *she* might be the twins' mother," whispered Kay.

There was a long silence before Amelia answered.

"We have had that very thought cross our minds," she sighed. "How that possibility could be true, though, is still undetermined. There are only three known Firemancy bloodlines. One of those bloodlines we can count out, as we are already familiar with their history."

"If it is somehow possible that *she* is their mother, what then?" asked Kanda.

"For now, nothing. Destiny has awakened their powers and their fate is already in motion. Of course, had we any inkling that Meghan was descended from a seer's bloodline, especially Firemancy, I do not know that we would have chosen to bind their powers when they were infants. Torture like this is certainly not what we intended for these youngsters once they encountered their destiny. Her power should have developed slowly over many years. Now, it comes on like a firestorm." She looked at Arnon pleading forgiveness.

"I did not know either," he replied. "I just wish there was more I could do."

Kanda squeezed his hand, smiling, weakly.

"Go to the boys," Kay told Arnon. "They will be going crazy by now waiting for news. We will stay with her tonight."

"Yes," agreed Kanda. "You know we will do everything we can for her. After all, we all think of her as our daughter, too."

Arnon could not argue with that. He left the trailer, trying to hold back tears.

Meghan tried to listen to the conversation going on around her. Exhaustion kept her from doing so, and she often went into and out of consciousness.

"Okay, ladies," said Kanda. "I have an idea of how to get Meghan through the next few days, but it is not going to be pleasant. The spells I have been using are already weakening and will not last. Her pain will keep intensifying."

"I think I know where you're going with this, which is why I insisted that Arnon leave," said Kay. "I do not think he could bear to see the amount of suffering Meghan will be in."

"Or the pain we will be in if my idea works," added Kanda.

Kay nodded with understanding.

"Bring it on then!" insisted Amelia, trying to sound courageous. "We can take turns and rest in between."

"I will take the first watch," said Kanda, her voice faltering. "I just hope this works. I fear that Meghan's body is not strong enough to pull through on her own."

"Then we will take on the highest amount of pain we can tolerate. We cannot lose this child," said a determined Amelia. "If our theories about her father's identity are true, then she is fated to be one of the three."

"Which makes us her path to that destiny," smiled Kay.

Kanda Macawi took a deep breath.

Almost as if directed, Meghan felt the pain returning. This time, however, along with the pain came strange visions. Pictures formed in her mind, but they dissolved into new ones so quickly that Meghan had no time to focus on them. Her eyes popped open and darted back and forth as if they were trying to read quickly. Her breathing sped up and then in the smallest of seconds, she stopped. Her eyes stared up at the ceiling of the trailer and the pain ended, and she held her breath.

Is it over? She dared think. A few seconds went by and Meghan slowly let out her breath, feeling no pain. She had not overheard everything that had been said, but she had heard enough to believe that whatever was happening to her was just beginning.

Then it happened. Meghan could not even scream. The visions returned and along with it, a burning so hot that she knew for sure she was actually burning alive. Her body thrashed on the sofa.

"We have to hurry," said Kanda, holding Meghan's hand. She heard Kanda take a deep breath, say something indiscernible and then cry out. Kay and Amelia were at her side in a second.

"I'm okay," she muttered, rocking back and forth. Kanda chanted quietly, focusing all her energy on taking as much of Meghan's pain and she could and transferring it to her own body. Her free hand remained in a tight fist. The two free women looked at each other, knowing that not too long in the future it would be their turn.

The visions in Meghan's head slowed and then stopped, one particular vision taking over, like a vivid dream that she could walk in, watching from the sidelines.

It was dark in the dream. Nighttime. She was standing outside of an old building, watching as three cloaked figures emerged. A sign over the door indicated it was an orphanage. The figures held two small, wrapped bundles.

"At least we found them first," whispered a man's voice.

"Yes," agreed another. "To show powers at such a young age. It is unheard of. They are lucky they did not cause any harm. Who knows what would have become of them."

"We should hurry," said a woman. "If it is true what they say, we do not want to be around if their father decides to show up."

The three, cloaked figures then disappeared into the darkness.

Chapter 6

Colin found himself sneaking into his sister's dreams again; they were vivid and strange. Unfortunately, along with seeing her dreams, he also felt her pain. More than once, Sebastien awakened him, afraid he was having nightmares.

"You can feel her, can't you?" he asked timidly, after the third time.

"I am not doing a good job at blocking her," Colin admitted.

"I take back anything I have ever said about what you two can do. Feeling someone else's pain, I could not handle that."

Colin did his best to block Meghan from his mind, but periodically she would sneak in. The night was long and fitful.

The warmth of the sun soon hit Colin's face and the smell of percolating coffee filled his nostrils. He rolled over, not ready to get up. He opened his eyes to Sebastien's face peering down at him.

"My mom is home and your uncle has just left."

Colin shook off his grogginess and bounded out of bed. Kay Jendaya appeared fatigued and worn; her husband helped her into the camper and she did not say a word to the boys. Sebastien's father stayed inside for a painfully long time. Finally, the door opened and the boys accosted him with questions. Mr. Jendaya shushed them and motioned to walk away from the camper.

"Kay needs to rest now. Meghan still has a fever, but is handling it like a trooper." He forced them to sit and eat breakfast. They hoped that Jae would arrive soon, with any news other than, 'she's handling it like a trooper'.

Half way through breakfast, Jae granted their wish. He sat down looking as tired as Sebastien's mother had. Colin was dying to talk to Jae, but had to wait until Mr. Jendaya was busy. At the end of breakfast, he told the boys he would clean up, and they should find something to keep themselves busy.

"But, by all means, stay away from that trailer!"

They had wanted to go to Jae's wagon, but would have to find another way. As they departed the Jendaya camp, Sebastien's father yelled out, "Oh, by the way. Happy birthday, Colin."

He had forgotten. He and his sister were now officially thirteen. Both Sebastien and Jae repeated the remark, though not as heartily. As soon as they had gone a safe distance, Jae stopped them.

"I am afraid I did not see much. There was a woman that I had not seen before."

"She must have been the doctor," said Colin. "What else?"

"Not much. I could not see Meghan."

"You should get some sleep," Colin told Jae.

"Nah. Couldn't sleep right now. I did nap a little in between watching out of my window." They set off for the lake, moodily skipping rocks, and sitting under the shade of the trees, quietly reflecting.

"She is seizing again," cried Amelia. "I'm sorry. I weakened and lost my concentration."

Kanda jumped from her seat and helped Amelia to her feet.

"It is harder than I thought it would be," she admitted shamefully.

"We are doing our best," Kanda reminded kindly. "I will take my turn now."

"You have not had a long enough rest," insisted Amelia. "I just need a moment."

Just then, Meghan bolted upright. The two women gently tried to push her down and keep her as still as possible. In the process, a thorn on Meghan's locket pricked her skin. She sank into a deep coma, feeling no more pain, hearing no more voices, and felt nothing.

Then, there *was* something. She opened her eyes, blinded by a great amount of light. Shadows formed as her sight slowly returned. She tried to stand, but the surface beneath her swayed, making her legs unstable. She fell to her knees and when she looked up, she could see. Everything was clear.

Her body bounced up and down, and Meghan realized she was kneeling on a petal of some kind. She stood up, slowly turning in circles, taking in her surroundings. *Roses?*

"Where am I?" she whispered. She decided to follow the stem of the rose bush, maneuvering around the thorns, some of which were nearly the size of her body.

A short distance later the path came to an opening in which two roses entwined each other, one black and one white. Underneath, a silvery feather floated, carrying the body of a sleeping woman. Meghan was not sure if she should try to wake the woman, whose face she could not see. Perhaps this woman could tell Meghan how to get home.

"Why exactly do I want to go home?" she muttered. "So I can be sick again?" She paused, closing her eyes, enjoying the complete silence and lack of burning pain. She sighed, opening her eyes. "I would still like to know where the heck I am."

She stepped closer to the woman, opening her mouth to speak. A tranquil voice stopped her.

"Do not awaken her yet. It is not time."

"Who are you? Where am I?" Meghan asked, looking around for the source of the voice.

"Fate has found you, my dearest Meghan," echoed the voice. "When the time is right, the lady on the feather will present herself to you."

"What do you mean?" asked Meghan, not understanding.

"There is much yet to learn before you are ready to meet her, Meghan. Patience my child."

Meghan's head began to grow fuzzy and she became unsteady. She stumbled, pricking herself once again on a nearby thorn.

The nothingness returned. The rose bush was gone.

The memory of the voice vanished.

Deep within a stone room, a middle-aged woman sat by her candles, her lifeline to the outside world, the world she had banished herself from many years before. Though her pale skin too often did not see the light of day, her beauty was stunning.

Each of her candles took the shape of a person or place she desired to watch over, and in the flames, she could see them. She could hear them. She could even talk to them if she so desired.

She desired the latter greatly, but her secret needed to remain so. Her heart ached to speak with those she had left behind, to explain why she had left them. However, giving in to that desire would render all she had worked for, and given up, useless.

"No! I will remain strong for those that I love. I will keep hope that one day they will see the truth and understand." She blew out her candles, plunging herself into darkness.

She wept, holding her face in her hands, longing for one more chance to hold her loved ones in her arms, to feel their embrace around her.

An unexpected light filtered through her wet fingers. She dropped her hands, assuming the candle of her self-made captor had lit. What did he want now?

When she looked more closely, she gasped, horror-struck.

"This is not possible!" she cried out. "What treachery is this?" She could answer her own question easily. It could not be a trick.

"These candles only obey one Firemancer. Me."

She crawled, hesitantly, to the newly lit candle, blowing off the thick layer of burning dust. The flame burned brighter. She had thought many times over the years of destroying the candle, but could not bring herself do it. Perhaps …

"No! She is dead! This cannot be!" She gazed into the flame, afraid to let herself believe for a moment that she could be alive. Nevertheless, there in the flame, was a redheaded girl, sleeping. The Firemancer's heart thumped rapidly, overflowing with emotion, which instantly turned to dread.

"He lied to me!" she whispered coarsely.

The Firemancer stood, unsure of what to do. Her breath came out in heavy waves. She wanted to flee, to give up, to avenge this deception. This changed everything!

She stopped herself before leaving the cave.

"This cannot change anything," she said painfully. "My plan is more necessary than ever before. Now, I cannot fail!"

The Firemancer fell to her knees sobbing tears of joy, watching the beautiful redheaded girl sleeping.

She was truly alive, and for now, this would have to be enough.

First a week passed, then nearly a second, with no new information. Meghan's condition was always the same: her fever would not break and she did not regain consciousness. Colin thought on occasion he heard her, calling out to him in his mind, but she never replied when he answered back.

Colin, wanting to comfort his very outwardly worried uncle, told him he sensed she was simply in a deep sleep, dreaming. Colin also hoped she would recover in time to say goodbye to Jae, who would be leaving in three days time. The blue moon was fast approaching.

That evening, hurried footsteps approached the Jendaya camp, scraping dirt as they hastened closer; the group waited breathlessly, hoping it was not bad news. Kay Jendaya came running into the firelight, out of breath and exhausted.

"The fever finally broke! She awoke for a short minute, then went back to sleep. She will be fine now." Uncle Arnon got up and headed for the trailer. Colin stood to follow. At first, he thought Uncle Arnon was going to say no.

"C'mon," he hastily decided, and they scurried away. Once inside the trailer, they saw her sleeping on the pull-out sofa.

Colin had never been this happy to see his sister. Arnon sat down, a look of relief on his face. Colin knelt next to the couch just gazing at her, waiting for her eyes to open. Minutes later, Colin's head drooped and his eyes closed. His head popped back up and his uncle forced him straight to bed without protest. As soon as his head hit the pillow, he fell into a deep sleep, not a dream in his head, just precious, wonderful, uninterrupted sleep.

A familiar voice rang through his thoughts the next morning.

"Colin, you awake?"

Colin jumped from his bunk and dashed out of the bedroom, to see Uncle Arnon handing Meghan a glass of juice. He grinned from ear to ear, rushing to her, hugging her hard, making her wince and spill her juice.

"Sorry," he said, laughing.

Tears streamed down their uncle's face.

"It's good to have you back," he said happily.

"What happened? How long have I been here? And why do I feel like I have been beat up?" She tried to sit up, but struggled. Uncle Arnon assisted her.

"It has been nearly two weeks," informed her uncle.

"What! That long?" Her memories of the previous two weeks were faint, like a distant dream she could not quite remember.

"You have been through a lot, Meghan. You had a terrible fever," he told her. "Do you remember anything?"

"I do remember the fever. There were times I thought I was literally burning alive. I remember seeing a lot of faces I did not recognize, and then, a lot of darkness, and a lot of lights, and something about roses." She shook it off and tried to gather her bearings. "Right now, I just feel great!" she added, smiling. "Like I wasn't even sick."

"I am going to run and tell everyone you are awake. They will be very relieved." As Arnon departed, Meghan saw her reflection in the window and quivered.

"Ugh, I am a mess. Hand me a brush, would you?"

Colin did so gladly. Minutes later, a troop of footsteps drew near the camper. "Oh, no," she cried from the bed. "He brought them all here, now. Look at me, I am in my night gown, and have not showered, in, ohhhhh," she cringed and hid under the covers.

The door flung open. First, appeared Mr. and Mrs. Jendaya, followed by Kanda Macawi, and then Sebastien, Jae, and Uncle Arnon. The camper was crowded with smiling faces. Meghan peeked her nose over the top of the covers at her audience, not sure of what to say.

"We will not stay long," insisted Kay. "We are just so relieved that you are better."

"Thank you," she murmured from behind the blanket.

"What are you doing?" asked her uncle.

"I look horrible," she whispered.

"She's already back to normal," laughed Sebastien.

"You have been sick for awhile," added Jae. "You are bound not to look your best."

This was not as helpful as he'd hoped it would be. Meghan disappeared under the blankets until everyone had left. Colin had to coax her out.

Though she had been out for nearly two weeks, she was surprised at how energetic she felt. She was ravenous, and Colin gladly made her breakfast. She then asked them to leave, insisting she was well enough to shower and dress. Uncle Arnon was nervous to leave her alone, but Colin reminded him he could sense if something was wrong, so he agreed.

Over an hour later, she finally materialized.

"I cannot believe it, but I am starving already," she told them. Arnon hopped into the trailer to make her another plate of food. She sat down next to Colin and minutes later gobbled down another plate.

"I think this evening," started Uncle Arnon, "will be time for a belated, although less lively than planned, birthday party."

"Wow. I even missed my thirteenth birthday," she moaned. Then she looked at Colin. "I messed up yours, too. Sorry," she squeaked in a regretful tone.

"We can make up for it tonight," he replied.

"Until then, young lady, I insist that you rest," Arnon ordered. She agreed, begrudgingly. A few hours later, after eating another plate of food at lunch, she pleaded for release from resting.

"I swear, Uncle Arnon. I will take it easy. I really feel fine. I think a walk would do me some good. You know, fresh air and all that."

Arnon thought on it for a few minutes before answering.

"Okay. Only if you promise to take it easy and Colin has to stay with you. I do not want you to be alone on your first full day of recovery."

She nodded yes and tried to keep her pace slow as she excitedly exited the trailer. The first thing they did was grab Jae and Sebastien.

"I cannot believe I was out for such a long time. Did anything happen?" she asked as they walked.

"You did not miss much," said Sebastien, standing close by her, concerned she might lose her balance, even though she looked steady on her feet.

"In a couple days you will be going home, Jae," said Meghan.

Jae seemed both happy and sad about this.

"Aren't you excited to be going home?" she questioned.

"Oh, of course. I miss my family." He then confessed, "It's just that, for the first time in my life I have been on my own." He hesitated before continuing. "It's a little hard to explain, but my magic is stronger. I can do things I couldn't do before and my spells last way longer too! I am ready to see my family, though," he added. "I am sure my mom is worried to death by now."

The mood did not stay dampened long, as a short while later it was time for the twins' belated thirteenth birthday party. It was a happy night. The adults sat around the fire partaking in a few cheerful spirits. Meghan, Colin, and Sebastien taught Jae how to play a card game called black queens, which he had unparalleled beginners luck at playing.

Meghan felt nearly back to normal, but started to get noticeably tired. The boys asked if she wanted to stop and get some rest, but she insisted they continue. In fact, Meghan was happier than she had ever remembered. Colin sensed this and could not help but grin. It was not often they were able to spend a night, surrounded by friends. They did not want it to end.

Colin awoke early the next morning. His happy feelings from the previous night vanished, as a strange sense of foreboding overcame him. He looked at his watch. He and Meghan were to meet up with Sebastien and Jae in a couple of hours to head into town, as the Blue Moon Festival was still in full swing.

Unable to sleep, he got up, dressed as quietly as he could, grabbed the Magicante, and headed to the lake. Colin understood Jae's desire for space. It was something he did not get a lot of, living in a small camper with two other people.

He combed the area hoping to find an empty swing, log, or rock near the water; but he was not the only early riser and they were all in use. He trekked onward, deeper into the woods. The pathway became narrow and muddy, growing quieter and darker. Voices resonated in front of him.

"Oh no. Not again," he sighed.

Colin slowed, unsure of whether he had time to run. In front of him, a large boy dropped from a tree branch and thudded onto the ground. Two others appeared, on each his right and left hand sides. Colin checked behind him and the path was still clear, however, he knew he could not outrun them.

"Where do you think *you're* going?" asked the head bully haughtily.

Colin did not answer.

The boy continued.

"Your sister isn't around to save you today, little Colin Jacoby."

And if I have anything to do with it, she won't! He tried to block his mind from hers, which was difficult under the present circumstances. More than anything, he wanted her to rest, and not be worried about him.

Colin backed up a step, still not speaking.

"Look at the boy who needs his sister to save him," the first toady taunted.

"Yeah, not so great now, are ya!" shouted the other. The head bully advanced closer, his vicious face right in front of Colin's, who trembled, but stood ready for whatever torture came next.

One of the boys pushed Colin down onto the muddy ground. The boys laughed and encroached in on him. Colin closed his eyes, waiting for the blows, or the mud, or for whatever embarrassing thing the boys could think of doing to him. A picture developed of the bullies freezing in place, giving him time to get away.

Meghan's voice came into his head.

"Colin, where are you? Are you in trouble?"

He did not answer her, but instead blocked her out, feeling foolish. He snuck a daring peek at the three boys, now standing over him. One held a mound of thick mud, heading for Colin's mouth.

When the boys hand was inches from his face, Colin yelled for them to stop, closing his eyes, expecting the mud to smother him.

When after a minute it did not, he glimpsed upward, squinting, in case they were biding their time, waiting for him to look up. When he opened his eyes, they nearly popped right out of their sockets. Colin jumped up, mud dripping down him, staring at the three boys, each frozen in place. The only thing they could move was their eyes and mouths.

"What's going on? I can't move my arms or legs," said the head bully. The other two could not formulate a full sentence and just screamed and whimpered.

Colin stepped closer.

"Did I do this?" he asked himself.

"What did you do to me?" cried the head bully. "You will regret this."

Comprehension started to dawn on Colin. Somehow, as with Meghan under the twisted oak tree, he had made magic happen all on his own. He wondered if he could do it again. He walked closer to the head bully, who instantly went quiet, his eyes following Colin's every move.

Colin was not sure exactly what to do, so he waved his hand around, but said nothing. This got the boys nervous again.

"Hey, what are you doing?" the head bully pleaded.

Colin concentrated carefully.

"Stop talking," he ordered.

At once, the three boys went silent. They still tried to talk, but nothing came out! Colin, both stunned and satisfied by the outcome, smirked, and said, "Take that!" He picked up the Magicante, which he had thrown onto a dry patch of ground, and sauntered on his way, leaving behind three confused and frightened boys.

As he walked, still astonished at what he had done, the screams of the boys returned. Colin's pace quickened. Gratifying as it was, he did not know if he could do it again.

Half way home, he ran into his sister, along with Sebastien and Jae. They saw him covered in mud, but grinning happily.

"Hey guys," he said cheerfully.

"What happened?" they all asked him, concerned and out of breath.

"Oh, I fell in the mud," he laughed. "Gonna go take a shower."

Meghan tried to read his mind, but he blocked her.

"I thought you said he was in trouble," said Sebastien.

"I thought he was. I guess he handled it." It came out as more of a question.

"That's good, right?" asked Jae.

"Yeah, I guess." Meghan was not sure what to think. Colin always needed her help to get out of trouble, why was today any different?

"You should not be exerting yourself that much yet anyway," said Sebastien.

Meghan's face went flush over his concern.

They headed back home where Uncle Arnon, Kanda Macawi and Sebastien's parents were getting ready to drive into town. They wanted Meghan to ride with them, but she insisted she was up to walking.

After Colin cleaned up, he, Meghan, Sebastien and Jae headed out of the camp. The festival was crowded with summer travelers, and the day flew by swiftly. While there, Colin glanced around, hoping to see Jasper Thorndike's tent set up again, but it was not there.

That evening, as the sun went down and the breeze cooled, they strolled jubilantly back to camp. Colin and Sebastien were busy watching Jae attempting to juggle, with Meghan lagging behind, happily amused.

Soon, they grew bored of Jae's attempts to juggle, so he used a spell to light the balls on fire. As he attempted to juggle the fiery orbs, Meghan found herself strangely attracted to the flames. Jae's attempt failed and the juggling balls scattered onto the dirt road. As Colin and Sebastien laughed over his failed attempt, Meghan's gaze followed one of the rolling balls. The flames drew her in and a shadow in the flame caught her eye.

How can I be seeing this?

In the flame, the shadow grew, until finally, she could decipher the image. It looked eerily similar to the road they were walking on right now, and she was nervously peering into to the sky. A figure appeared in the sky, and began to dive.

They were under attack!

Two Scratchers dove at them, knocking them to the ground.

Blood!

It spread over the ground creating a crimson pool.

Meghan inhaled deeply, as if she was taking her very first breath and then her trance ended and the image disappeared.

"Meghan, are you okay?" asked Colin, as Jae put out the flames. Sebastien pulled at her arm when she did not answer. She stared blankly, wondering what the vision had meant. Her heart stopped for a brief moment, as she dared believe what her gut was telling her.

Was it really a warning?

But how?

There was no time!

She struggled to find her voice, but all that would come out was a frightened whisper.

"Run. Now!"

Colin, Sebastien and Jae stared, bewildered. She looked at the three of them with an ominous gaze, her legs unable to move.

It was too late.

A shadow flew overhead.

A low snarl filtered through the thick pines. Sebastien was the only one *not* to understand, yet.

A second shadow flew over them.

The four huddled together, looking upward. The air was silent, not even a breeze swayed high up in the trees.

"Colin," started Jae.

Colin jerked up his head, blocking his thoughts from Meghan. *Why does he want me? Did he find out what I did? How could he? I can't fight Scratchers, a couple of bullies, maybe.* He answered hesitantly. "Yeah, Jae?"

"Don't suppose you have that nifty old book with you?"

He did not!

It was the first time he had left the trailer without it.

"What do we do, Jae?" breathed Meghan, trying to ignore the pool of blood, still fresh in her mind from her fiery vision.

"How many are there?" asked Sebastien, wisely picking up what was happening. There were now five flying ominously overhead.

"I wish you hadn't forgotten that book," squealed Meghan.

"Sorry," was all Colin could muster.

"No, this is my fault," said Jae.

The other three gaped at him.

"I should have been prepared for this. The blue moon is tomorrow. I dropped my guard."

Sebastien stood up tall.

"Just tell us what to do, we will be fine," he said. Meghan flicked her head to look at Sebastien. Was it his blood she had seen? There had to be a way to stop her vision from coming true.

"For now," said Jae. "Stay close. Let's keep moving." They proceeded slowly, watching the shadows fly overhead. A high-pitched, shriek-filled howl cut into the air.

"C'mon, this way," urged Jae. "Stay together." The shrieking grew closer and the foursome started to run. Sebastien grasped Meghan's hand, helping her along.

Seconds later the foursome fell forward onto the ground, as a webbed wing of one of the Scratchers knocked them over. The group got up and scampered out of the way, as another of the Scratchers came diving down for a second swipe. Meghan, Colin and Sebastien ducked out of its way, but one of its claws grazed Jae's shoulder. He screamed and fell. The other three ran to his aid.

"I'm fine," said Jae. "It's not deep." It may not have been deep, but it bled heavily. Jae left behind a bloody puddle as he got up.

Meghan hoped desperately that this was the all the blood that would be shed.

Two Scratchers flew high overhead and the other three circled the foursome, creating a forceful wind each time their wings beat against the air. The creatures howled and clicked, as if talking to each other, planning their attack.

Jae pushed through the other three, rushing forward. He held out his hand, palm forward.

"Emissio!" he yelled furiously.

A blast of heavy air broke the circle, forcing the Scratchers to retreat, but only long enough for the foursome to run a short distance down the road. Another dove, separating the group and knocking Sebastien to the ground. He picked up his head in time to see another of the Scratchers diving.

"Meghan, behind you!" he warned.

Colin heard Sebastien yell and watched as the claws of the creature opened wide and enclosed around his sister, lifting her off the ground.

Jae raced to Sebastien's side.

"We cannot let it wrap its wings around her."

"What happens then?" Colin asked, afraid of the answer.

"She'll die!" Jae confirmed.

Colin watched the Scratcher lifting Meghan's body higher off the ground, thankfully not in the right position to be wrapped in its wings.

Jae furiously talked to himself, trying to figure out what to do.

"I've got it!" he suddenly shouted. "I'm gonna do a spell to pull it forward." Before Jae had the chance, the remaining Scratchers had them surrounded.

Meghan was now fifteen feet in the air, kicking and trying to free herself.

Colin's mind was overwrought with fear and something inside him changed. From his toes to his fingertips, he felt a power surging through him. A power so strong he was afraid he might explode if he did not use it.

"Jae," he yelled, "I will hold these ones off," he said firmly. "You get my sister back!"

Jae started to question him, when Colin interrupted.

"Just go." Colin faced the circling Scratchers. His knees shook uncontrollably. Hoping he had not made the biggest mistake of his life, and not being sure if he was doing it right, he faced his palm outward.

"Emissio!" he shouted. He could feel the energy raging through his body pouring into his palm, but nothing happened. He planted his feet firmly against the ground, taking a deep breath to calm himself.

"Emissio," he repeated.

This time, the force of energy was so strong he could barley keep his feet planted on the ground.

It worked!

The creatures retreated.

Behind him, both Sebastien and Jae watched in electrified awe. A scream from Meghan regained their attention. The Scratcher was struggling to hold onto her and she was now grasping *it* firmly, trying not to plummet to the ground far below.

"I'm going to try and pull it down, Sebastien. When I do, grab her, and hold tight."

"That's your plan?" yelled Sebastien. "Grab her!"

Jae ignored him, focused on his task.

"Valeerea," shouted Jae, his hand shaking. The spell caught the beast, causing him to howl viciously, nearly dropping Meghan, again.

Behind them, Colin repeated his spell. The Scratchers backed off, also strangely appearing caught off guard by Colin's use of magic.

Jae pulled his imprisoned creature toward Sebastien. Every muscle in his body raged with power and the fortitude not to give up. He exhausted so much magical energy that his appearance-changing spell stopped working. His normal stringy hair returned, hiding his determined eyes.

Sebastien could see Meghan's strength waning.

"Hold on Meghan! I can almost reach you," he shouted. Her legs dangled in the air as the flying beast held onto her by her shoulders; its claws digging in. Meghan tried to force the claws out of her, but she was too weak. She dangled four feet from the ground now, which meant that the creature's wings were a danger to Sebastien.

"Grab her now, Sebastien!" instructed Jae, beginning to tire. Sebastien took hold as tight as he could to her legs. Jae took his free left hand and yelled (still holding the right one strongly), "Emissio!"

The creature, clearly in torment, let go of Meghan. Sebastien carefully swung her to the ground and cupped his body over hers, protecting her from the creatures floundering wings, as it struggled to remain airborne.

A sharp claw scratched the entire length of Sebastien's back. Meghan was terrified that Sebastien was seriously injured, but he kept his place protecting her, insisting he was fine.

Jae could no longer hold both spells. He let go and collapsed, exhausted.

Colin stopped his own spell and rushed to Jae's side.

The four got up and with every ounce of strength they had left, ran, leaving the Scratchers flying above, reorganizing for another attack.

"Hurry," said Jae. "If we can get to the entrance, where there are people, I don't think they'll follow."

"Can you be sure?" asked Meghan, leaning on Sebastien's arm for support.

"I am not sure about anything anymore," he replied, as they ran. They did not stop until they came into view of people; people completely oblivious to the danger that lurked overhead.

Children played kickball in the wide park entrance. Two runners left the campground, running in the opposite direction of the foursome, who left the roadway a few feet before the entrance, seeking the coverage of the trees and bushes. Once out of sight they crumpled to the ground. After a few minutes of catching their breath and gathering their thoughts, Meghan jumped up.

"Sebastien! Your back!"

"I think its okay, it doesn't hurt much."

She made him roll over and to everyone's relief, the claws had gone through his shirt, but had not broken through his skin. A long swollen scratch etched from his right shoulder to his lower back. There was no blood.

Jae wanted to heal everyone's injuries, but he needed time to recover. He turned to Colin.

"I guess I could let you try it, Mr. Magic Man," he said pompously. Colin knew he had some explaining to do, but had no idea where to begin. The other three waited for his explanation. Colin sensed Meghan trying to break into his thoughts.

"Will you give me a second?" he said aloud to her.

"Sorry," she replied impatiently.

"Don't *you* have some explaining to do, too?" he questioned. This was true, but Colin continued anyway. "I am not sure how it happened. Maybe it has got something to do with my new book."

"Why didn't you tell me?" Meghan asked angrily. "You did not think you could hide it from me did you?"

"You are just getting over being sick, and I didn't know how to tell you."

"Has this ever happened to you before?" asked Jae, with growing bewilderment and concern.

"Only since I bought the Magicante."

"But that book was not with you today," reminded Sebastien.

"Maybe it was working long distance?" Colin suggested, somewhat sarcastically.

"Perhaps," said Jae, eying Colin with a new-found wonder.

Now it was Meghan's turn. The three boys waited for her to explain how she knew the attack was coming. She now blocked her thoughts from Colin, trying to muster an explanation.

The only problem was, she did not understand it herself.

"I..." she stopped, and then said, "It was just intuition." She knew that was a bad answer. Jae raised his eyebrow, clearly not believing her. Colin knew his sister was lying. Then again, he had not really told the truth either.

"Regardless of whatever is happening with the sudden breakout of magical powers," said Sebastien. "We should probably get closer to home."

"We certainly cannot go back looking like this!" said Jae. It appeared as though they had been in a mini war. Their clothes were torn and their bodies caked with dirt and mud. Plus, all of them, minus Colin, had injuries from the creatures' sharp talons.

"Since our injuries are small, I think I can fix them," he said. "Everyone stand close by each other." He waved his hand and said something inaudible for the rest to hear. In an instant their clothes mended, the mud vanished and their wounds healed. He did the same thing to himself, and then redid his appearance spell.

"I can't believe I just did all that after a battle," he said as they departed the woods. "My powers never renew so easily."

Their gazes grazed the skyline as they walked deeper into the campground.

Meghan was deep in thought, and Sebastien, walking beside her, tried to feel his back, not believing the scratch had vanished. Jae held back, walking alongside Colin.

"I wish I wasn't leaving tomorrow night. I would like some more time to look over that book again."

"Do you think you could learn anything about it?"

"Dunno, but you guys have helped me out a ton. I wish I could return the favor." There was silence between them for a moment, before Jae added, "However you did it, Colin, that was an awesome show of force. It took me years of practice to do that. Whatever you do, be careful. You do not want to make any enemies."

"You mean, like the Scratchers?"

"Exactly like the Scratchers."

They were silent the rest of the way home.

"What do we do now?" asked Meghan, as they approached their uncle's trailer.

"We go home and pretend that nothing happened," proposed Sebastien, catching on quickly to the secret filled, magical lifestyle.

"Sounds about right," frowned Jae.

"I think I could get used to this magic thing," boasted Colin.

Meghan rolled her eyes, half-amused at his daring behavior, and half-afraid of what it meant.

A fire lit up the Jacoby campsite. Meghan did not trust the fire, unsure of what would happen if she looked into the flames. When she did finally dare to cast a glance, the flames cast no shadows or visions, just warmth.

"There you are, we were going to come searching for you all," said Milo Jendaya. "We thought you might have gotten lost," he joked.

They sat around the warm fire, thankful for the option not to speak, and simply stared blankly into the flames. Meghan and Colin eventually linked their minds.

"I am nervous about tomorrow," said Meghan. "What if something goes wrong and Jae does not get home."

"He has to," replied Colin.

"At least you can fight those things off if we need to get away, and you better remember that book this time." Colin was not fond of the idea of fighting again, with magic at his side or not! His heart quickened at the thought.

"I will remember the book, but what if I can't do that again, fight them I mean?"

Meghan sensed his fear.

"Thanks, Colin."

"For what?" he asked her.

"I know you, and what you did was, well, brave. If you had not tried it, I don't want to think where I might be right now, or if I would even still... be."

Colin's face went pink. A compliment from Meghan. Brave. Him?

Once again, they lost themselves in the flames. Jae announced he was going home and said goodnight. Meghan, Colin, and Sebastien watched as he walked away, for what *should* be his last night with them. It made them sad, but also scared that something might go wrong.

Colin dozed off, leaning his head against his chair. Sebastien and the Jendayas departed. Uncle Arnon awoke the dozing Colin and marched him into the trailer.

"I will put out the fire tonight, Uncle Arnon," offered Meghan.

"Are you sure you're feeling up to it?"

"Yeah, it's actually very relaxing."

"Okay then. Just be careful."

Meghan poked around, breaking up the burning embers, when something caught her eye, something moving in the fire. She stepped back, with the poker raised in her hand, ready to strike.

"What is this now?" she asked herself, wondering if perhaps she was just jumpy and had not actually *seen* anything.

Something jumped out of the fire pit, darting to the edge. Meghan stepped back, aghast, as it meowed at her. It was a cat, with one white eye and one black eye. It had a slim body covered in fine, almost non-existent hair, similar to a Siamese cat.

"Who are you and what do you want?" Meghan asked boldly, realizing she was asking a cat to reply to her question. Then again, it did just jump out of a lit fireplace. Meghan gasped when the cat did respond, actually speaking to her.

"My master wants to meet you Meghan Chelcy Jacoby," a cattish, girly voice said.

"Your m-master," Meghan had only heard this term used in movies. "And why should I do that?" she asked, keeping her distance.

"Do not ask why. It is a great honor to be asked, little girl."

"Little girl!" Meghan repeated, edging closer to the strange cat. "Now look here, you," she said a little louder, blocking her mind from her brother, hoping not to raise any suspicion from inside the trailer. "I am not a little girl."

The cat hissed and meowed back at her.

"You can tell your master that I'm not interested! *What am I doing?*" she berated herself. "Having an argument with a cat? What's next?"

Meghan realized that she was so close to the fire pit she was nearly touching it, and was surprised that it did not feel hot, but rather quite comfortable.

"Suit yourself," the cat hissed, pawing at her. "My master may choose to come and visit you, then!"

"Visit here? Why?"

Maybe she was putting Colin's and her uncle's lives in danger by not going with this menacing cat. Maybe this master person could answer some questions about what was happening to her and Colin.

She stepped closer to the cat, within its reach now, her legs touching the fire pit.

"Why should I go with you? Will I be able to get home?"

"You will have to trust me," it trilled.

"And why should I trust you?"

"I'm leaving. You can either come with me, or stay here," it purred. Meghan's eyes rolled anxiously to her family in the trailer, and then back to the cat.

"To come, you simply take hold of me."

"I'll burn myself!" Somehow, she knew this was not true.

"I do not think so," said the cat. "You and fire, let's just say, get along extremely well."

Meghan leaned in and grasped hold of the cat's back.

"Hold on, it may be a rough ride."

The cat began to dissolve into the fire, and Meghan's arm fell into the burning embers; it was a strange sensation, but it did not burn.

Something grabbed her from behind, pulling her out of the fire. The cat meowed viciously, dissolving fully into the flames. Meghan fell back and landed on someone. She rolled over onto the ground.

"What do you think you're doing?" she asked, before looking.

Jae's voice answered, startling her.

"Saving you from that Catawitch." He helped her up.

"You know what that thing is?" she asked him.

"Yes, I caught a glimpse of it from my window. I ran over as fast as I could. You do not want to mess with a Catawitch until you are positive what its true motives are. They are loyal to their masters, good or bad."

"But why would it want *me*? It said its master wanted to meet me."

Jae was instantly alarmed.

"Its master wanted to meet you?" he was silent for a moment. "This is strange, Meghan. You see, those cats rarely come out of the magical world, they do not belong in this one."

"That thing is from the magical world?" she asked.

"Yes. They are magical cats, loyal only to their masters; so loyal, that they can even give up one of their lives to save them from death."

"Now that's a heck of a cat!" exclaimed Meghan. "But that does not explain why it wanted me to come with it."

"No, it doesn't. But I would guess it has something to do with what's been happening to you and your brother." He paused again, and advising, "I would ignore it if it returns."

Meghan did not think she would care to go, and was glad she had not.

"Thanks for stopping me," she said to Jae.

"It is the least I can do after all your help. It certainly has not been boring around here."

"It is odd you say that, Jae, because before we met you, things were always boring around here. None of these bizarre things ever happened."

"Maybe after I leave things will go back to normal," he said, trying to convince himself that his new friends would be safe once he had left. "See you tomorrow," he said, vanishing into the darkness.

"Yeah, tomorrow," she replied, feeling even more overwhelmed.

She *was* hopeful that Jae would get home the next night, but her mind was full of doubt. Why were all these strange things happening? Moreover, what was this new problem of the Catawitch, as Jae had called it? Why was the magical world, which they had only just discovered existed, sneaking its way into their boring, normal world?

Inside the trailer, Colin could not hear Meghan's thoughts, but similar unanswered questions raced through his own mind.

There were no answers.

Later, Colin and Meghan lay in bed, both awake, and both hiding their confused thoughts from each other. Eventually they drew the same conclusion. Whatever was happening to them would have to wait. Tomorrow was a big day. Tomorrow, they had to be sure that Jae Mochrie returned to his caravan, safe, alive and preferably in one once piece.

Chapter 7

The twins lay in bed early the next morning, having not slept at all. They did not speak or get out of bed right away. Hearing movement in the kitchen, they knew their uncle was awake. Meghan knew she should make breakfast, and dragged herself out of bed.

"Colin, what's happening to us?" she asked him unexpectedly. She did not sound scared, but puzzled. He had been up most of the night thinking about the same subject.

"No idea, Sis. It is a peculiar feeling, though. I feel different, but not wrong." He shrugged, realizing his explanation did not make a lot of sense.

Meghan had not yet told him about the Catawitch from the previous night. She took a deep breath and started.

"Not that this helps answer anything, but last night, another *unusual* thing happened."

"When?" he asked.

"While I was putting out the fire," she explained. "I had a visitor. One I am guessing was

185

not a friendly foe." She told him about the cat appearing in the fire and asking her to go with it to meet its master, how she had almost gone when it threatened Colin and Uncle Arnon, and how it did not hurt her when she touched the fire.

"What stopped you from going with the Catawitch?"

"Jae. He was the one that told me it *was* a Catawitch. He also said it was a creature from the magical world."

"Magical world?" he questioned. "But why?"

"I'm not sure, but I have been thinking about it, and I believe it might have something to do with Jae. All these things started during the time we met him."

"And Jae did hint at more enemies out there than just the Scratchers," reminded Colin.

"Maybe they are trying to use us, to get to Jae, or his people?" suggested Meghan.

"How can we be sure? What can we even do about it?"

"I think we need to hope that things go back to normal once Jae is gone. I also think Jae might be in a lot more danger than he's led us to believe," said Meghan.

"But the Catawitch's visit and Jae being in danger, still doesn't fully explain what has been happening to us," said Colin, with an inquisitive look on his face. "There has to be some kind of explanation or connection."

"Colin," said Meghan apprehensively. "What if that book was not meant for you, but for Jae. Perhaps someone trying to help him. We don't really know that much about him when it comes down to it. Maybe he was not as alone as we thought."

It had not crossed Colin's mind that the book was not meant for him.

"Jasper Thorndike seemed quite keen on *me* having this book." He thought for a few minutes more, before saying, "Magicante did help us escape from those Scratchers, before Jae got stuck behind."

"That's true. Maybe someone wanted to help us then, knowing Jae and the Svoda would bring trouble with them."

"But who? And why?" he asked. Colin then had a depressing thought.

"How do we know that when Jasper Thorndike sold me Magicante, he was not trying to hurt them? We would have been an easy, unsuspecting target! We could have put Jae in danger and not even realized it!" He snatched up Magicante and asked it, "Are you using us to try and hurt someone?"

The only response was the sound of interrupted snoring.

"Was worth a try," he shrugged.

"I don't think the book was meant to harm anyone, although, it is rude enough. I *do* think Jae might believe something could use us as a target, and I would bet that is why he is still watching us from his wagon window."

"Has he been?" asked Colin.

"That is how he saw me talking to the Catawitch."

Colin gazed sadly at his book, looking forlorn.

"I will miss Jae, too," she said. "Whatever he's not telling us, or protecting us from, I hope he makes it home safely."

"Oh, I do hope he makes it home," agreed Colin. "I was just thinking that doing magic is incredible. I guess I am hoping it will stick around after Jae's gone."

He drew back his curtain so he could be alone, attempting to hide his disappointment. Colin sulked in his chair thinking back to how he had been able to stop the bullies, and trusting that after tonight, it would not happen again. At that moment, he did not feel strong or powerful. Just the same old version of himself, who always needed his sister to come to his rescue.

Meghan left the room to prepare breakfast, but discovered her uncle had beaten her to it. It was ready and on the table. Colin did not come out until thirty minutes later and appeared sluggish when he did.

"Bad night's sleep?" questioned his uncle.

"You could say that," he groaned.

"You two have had some long days and late nights. I think an early night is in order tonight." He added, "Need to get your rest. Rest revives your energy and you both seem short on it this morning. Yup, early to bed tonight."

The twins gawked at each other. Had he guessed they were planning to sneak out again? They knew they were facing a major grounding in order to help Jae.

Unease overshadowed the rest of the breakfast as their fears intensified. Mostly, they feared getting caught, and Uncle Arnon not allowing them to leave, and Jae being on his own against the Scratchers.

After finishing their morning chores, they headed out to meet Jae and ran into Sebastien.

"You look as bad as we do," Colin attempted to joke.

"Speak for yourself there Bro," said Meghan.

"I hope Jae slept better than we did. Let's get over there!" suggested Sebastien.

Jae greeted them at the wagon door, and to their astonishment, he looked rested and awake.

"You guys look awful," he told them.

Meghan took special offense.

"A little tired maybe," she commented.

Colin and Sebastien gave Jae a sign *to not go there.*

Jae changed the subject. "What should we do on my last day here?"

"Do?" Meghan said bombastically. "How do we know that as soon as we go anywhere, to DO anything that those Scratchers won't be out there?"

Jae could see they were all worried about this. He made an announcement, one he thought would help.

"I have made a decision."

They listened eagerly.

"When the time comes tonight, I will go alone."

At once, the three of them disagreed, arguing the point as to why they should accompany him. He let them continue for a few minutes, before finally interrupting.

"If I am alone, less can go wrong. I would bet my life that my dad will be coming for me, and, I think it is best if I am there alone. I have not exactly mentioned it before, but the Svoda are not always kind to strangers. They will not approve if I'm standing there with three people who obviously know about our magic. Our secret."

They realized that for Jae's long-term safety, this might be necessary, but it did not make them any happier about promising.

"Are there more than just the Scratchers out there hunting the Svoda?" asked Meghan, hoping to have at least one question answered. Jae bowed his head, and took a long time before answering.

"I do not dare say too much, but yes," he sighed.

"Oh. I can't imagine living with constant fear of being hunted."

"That is why I have to go alone, otherwise..." Jae stopped.

"Otherwise, what?" asked Colin, leaning in closer.

"Otherwise, they will make you forget you ever met me!"

"That's possible?" asked Meghan, alarmed.

"Yes, and they will do it if they find out. When it comes down to it, I have been breaking many rules. Really, there was no way around it. But they will not see it that way, and I do not want you guys to forget, because maybe someday our paths will cross again."

"Will you get into trouble if you are caught breaking the rules?" asked Sebastien.

"Yes, another reason to keep the secret. If anything ever got back to our Banon, Juliska Nandalia Blackwell, well let's just say it would be a majorly ugly situation!"

"Banon?" questioned Meghan.

"Our leader. You two must have seen her. She was there the night I got stuck behind."

Meghan recalled the woman, instantly.

"She fought the Scratchers. I liked her style."

"Now I remember," said Colin. "Scratchers were looming overhead, people were disappearing into a pine tree, and she remembers how stylish the woman was."

The boys laughed.

Meghan scowled.

"She just seemed to be with it, and beautiful to boot." It did not help her cause.

"She is definitely *with it.* She has held her position longer than any other Banon, and many Svoda are stricken by her beauty!"

"Humpf," was all Meghan said, now annoyed.

"One cannot help it I suppose," Jae continued, oblivious to Meghan's escalating temper. "She is possibly the most beautiful Svoda woman, ever."

"I'm getting out of here," huffed Meghan, stomping her way out of the wagon. *I will never understand boys.* She recalled the woman, the Banon of the Svoda, with an odd fascination.

"Juliska Nandalia Blackwell," she spoke it aloud. The name had a regal ring to it. A few minutes later, the boys exited the wagon. She still had an annoyed look on her face and sat waiting, but they were not sure for what. Colin searched through her mind, trying to pick up what she wanted; it finally hit him.

"Apologize? For what?"

Sebastien and Jae stood off to the side, waiting for an explanation.

Meghan sighed and nodded her head in annoyance. It was now late morning and the day was disappearing quicker than she had anticipated. In her mind, she went over the things she *should* be taking care of. The laundry was piling up. Uncle Arnon needed a zipper fixed on a pair of jeans.

None of these normal duties mattered to her today. They seemed mundane and pointless.

"Let's go down to the lake," she suggested, already taking off. The three boys followed, shaking their heads behind her, muttering, "Girls," and making crazy motions with their fingers against their heads.

The lake was crowded and loud, which was a rare pleasantry since none of the youngsters desired to talk. They waded in the water, skipped rocks and wasted away the day. With every minute that passed, Meghan, Colin and Sebastien grew more anxious for Jae, and as evening approached, Jae poorly hid his own rising concerns.

Clouds rolled in, covering the warm sun that had followed them all afternoon. A cool breeze followed, and then it began to drizzle. Fog rolled across the lake hiding most of it from view and patches of it hid the ground along their pathway home.

Colin protected his book, which he had kept with him all day, hidden under his sweater, just in case. Part way back to camp, one of Kanda's caretakers was burning a large pile of brush.

"Gotta wait for a rainy day to get a permit," he reveled in the irony. The foursome enjoyed the fire, but after a minute, Sebastien and Jae went and sat on a nearby rock, saying the heat was too much for them. Colin shortly followed. Meghan thought it was perfect and could have moved closer. When she tried, the manager peeked around the corner.

"Don't be gettin' too close, little lady," he warned. "May be damp out here, but clothes can still catch."

She stepped back, shivering. In a split second, the flames pulled her back in. The Catawitch was back, staring at her from inside the fire.

"Hello Meghan. Did not think I forgot you now, did you?" it purred.

"Like that's possible," she mumbled back. "What do you want?"

"You know what I want, and you know you want to."

"You don't know anything!" she boasted too loudly, seizing the attention of the manager. He stepped around the corner of the fire.

"All right there, little lady?"

Meghan nodded yes, hoping he would not come any closer and scare away the Catawitch.

"What do you really want?" Meghan asked as soon as it was safe. "Are you using me to get to someone else?" She decided to speak bluntly.

"Someone else," it purred. "Like who, your brother or dear old uncle? Maybe your best friend, Sebastien?" it purred more loudly. "Or, perhaps your new friend, Jae? Ah, wouldn't you like to know." It snarled at her, stepping closer.

Meghan was so close to the fire now she was afraid the manager might come and pull her away.

"Come and you will see. My master will show you."

"Who is your master?"

Before the Catawitch could reply, the camp manager yanked Meghan backwards. She did not realize that she had fully stepped into the fire. The boys, now seeing what was happening, flew to her side. The Catawitch was gone. Disappointment covered her face. The manager looked over her arms, which were completely unharmed by the fire.

"You're mighty lucky, little lady, not a burn on ya." He was clearly shaken. "Better be more careful, might not be so lucky next time."

The boys briskly whisked her away before the manager could ask any questions.

Jae scolded her, harshly.

"He is right! You *should* be more careful. You could have been hurt, or worse."

"I was standing near the fire. Okay, a little too close."

"How about in the fire, Meghan. Uh, how did you do that exactly?" asked her brother.

"It's the same as last night. I think it is because of the Catawitch," she admitted, not quite believing that was the entire truth.

"It was back, just now?" Jae confirmed hastily, glancing back at the now distant fire.

"Yes," she answered, remembering that Sebastien did not understand what they were discussing. He was about to ask when she broke in, explaining.

Jae was gravely concerned. What would happen to his new friends after his departure?

"Meghan," he said, after she'd finished. "Promise me something, will you?" He looked her straight in the eye, his old arrogance returning. "After I leave, if the Catawitch comes back, ignore it! Do not even talk to it. It cannot harm you or take you anywhere unless you go willingly." He turned to Colin. "I expect you to watch her until this Catawitch decides to leave her alone."

He clearly did not trust Meghan to listen to him, which angered her. And she certainly didn't need a babysitter, especially if it was Colin. She stormed off but Sebastien seized her arm, stopping her. She faced him eye to eye, recognizing something she had never seen before... fear.

"I think this is important, Meghan."

She did not speak, but gawked awkwardly at the three boys, growing infuriated. She kept walking. No one stopping her this time.

"Why does everyone suddenly think they need to tell me what to do? I have always done just fine on my own," she muttered crossly. Her stomach was ill and she hated that she had not found out what the Catawitch wanted.

What if it did come back?

What would she do?

Could she ignore something that might want to harm her, her family, or her friends?

What if the Catawitch did not mean any harm? Jae had said they were not evil cats, just loyal to their masters.

No. She knew if she followed her gut, that it did not have good intentions. She found herself back at her uncle's trailer, but with no desire to go inside. Tears filled her eyes and she slumped down letting the rain drizzle over her face; it did not hide the fact that she was crying. She heard the boys enter Jae's wagon. Colin's thoughts perplexed her.

"No, I think we should let her be. You can't talk to her when she gets like this."

"Like this! What is that supposed to mean?" Behind her, the trailer door opened and Kanda Macawi climbed down the steps. Meghan hastily wiped her face, but her smudged makeup easily gave her away.

Her uncle waved Meghan into the trailer and out of the rain but she ignored him. It was impossible for Meghan to hide. Kanda had already spotted her.

"Get yourself together," Meghan said. "This isn't like you."

"Hello, Meghan," greeted Kanda. "I dropped off an old radio I am hoping Arnon can fix. If anyone can…" she saw Meghan's face and plopped down, putting an arm around her shoulder. "What, may I ask, is the cause of this?" she asked, genuinely concerned.

"It's nothing, I'm fine," squeaked out Meghan.

"Meghan, I have seen plenty of tears in my day. Tears do not happen for *no* reason." She took out a tissue and dabbed Meghan's wet face. She could not answer; the words would not come out. Instead, a torrent of uncontrollable tears erupted.

Meghan despised it.

It was weak.

Kanda hugged her and let the tears fall. After a few minutes, she was finally able to stop the tears and regain some control. Kanda did not ask her to speak, but sat patiently as Meghan blew her nose.

"Thanks," she said, throwing the tissue into the rain soaked fire pit.

"It was nothing. Honestly, I almost decided to join you. Sometimes there is nothing like a good cry. Somehow I feel better after, renewed."

As Meghan thought about it, she did feel better.

"I wish there were another way. Crying sucks," she admitted.

"So why were you, if you want to talk about it?"

"I dunno. A lot of reasons. Everything's changing."

"Oh, I see. Change is bound to happen."

"But that doesn't make it any easier."

"Meghan, you are growing up and so is your brother. People change. You cannot expect things to stay the same forever." It was one of those statements grown ups were known to make. Meghan considered herself already quite grown up, but still did not see why anything should have to change.

"Meghan, my sweet child, if I may be honest," Kanda began.

Meghan feared what she would say, but it was not what she expected.

"You have had a hard life, traveling from place to place, losing your parents before you could even remember them. Plus, you seem to be under the impression you can control everything about your life. Do not think it has gone unnoticed how you take care of your brother when he is in trouble, or worry about your uncle. You've had to take on many responsibilities, far beyond most girls your age."

Meghan's perplexed face made it clear she had never thought about it that way before.

"My point is, have a good little cry over it. But please, remember, sometimes you have to look out for yourself too."

Meghan was speechless.

"Look, it's getting colder and you are soaked," said Kanda. "We do not need you getting sick again, so why don't you get warmed up and dried off. Come by tomorrow and we will have a tonic, or some hot tea, if it persists on raining."

It had been awhile since Meghan had visited Kanda. Her teas were always soothing.

"Yeah, okay," she agreed.

Kanda reached over and hugged her. It was a deep, warm kind of hug, one that you could disappear and hide in. Meghan stiffened a little, not being used to that kind of a hug. Kanda let go and stood up to leave. The drizzle had wilted her hair and was collecting on her sweater.

"If events start to seem overwhelming, Meghan," she started, "there is only one place to look." Kanda placed her hand over her heart. "It will guide you through the muck and confusion."

Meghan was confident that her heart was causing most of her confusion. She sat a little longer, watching Kanda's figure disappear around the corner. It was the first time she had ever had a grown up type conversation, and although she felt better, she still did not want things to change. She definitely did not want to worry her uncle. It seemed he always had enough to worry about for the three of them.

Chapter 8

Evening had arrived. Meghan cleaned up her face and headed for Jae's wagon, determined to salvage the rest of the day. The boys were at the table. They stared at her unsure of what to say. She sat down, opened a tonic, with an air about her that said *you're the crazies, not me.*

"So what is your plan for tonight, Jae?" asked Colin after awhile.

"Pretty simple. Gonna head out about half hour before midnight, stay hidden, and then when the doorway opens, go home."

"And what if something *does* go wrong?" challenged Meghan.

"Don't worry, I won't be alone. As I said, I am sure my dad will be there, maybe more. They will fight off the Scratchers if they show. It will all go perfect."

Sebastien raised his bottle of tonic.

"A toast then, to our departing friend."

"And our lives getting back to normal," added Meghan.

"To hoping maybe a little magic sticks around once you're gone," Colin muttered timidly.

Jae raised his bottle clinking it against the others.

"To my new friends! I hope we meet again."

They downed the tonic, which bubbled and stung their throats. Sebastien was the first to finish and belched loudly and proudly. Meghan swished her hand across her nose, choking over hers. Colin could do little better than tiny sips at a time. Jae guzzled his and slammed the bottle down.

The sun was fading fast.

"Do you want to have dinner with us, Jae?" asked Meghan.

"I need to rest, save my strength for later. Just in case," he added at the end, seeing their untrusting faces. They said their goodbyes, hugging and patting each other on the back. Jae waved to the trio as they departed, somberly.

Sebastien walked the twins to their camp and joined them around the fire. Uncle Arnon had dinner simmering over the fire pit and glanced oddly at the gloomy trio as he stirred the pot. Meghan, noticing her uncle's stares busied herself setting the dinner table, and ordered Colin to help. The last thing they needed was for him to question their somber demeanor.

Every few minutes their eyes drifted toward Jae's soon to be deserted wagon. In between their worried gazes, they listened for any sign of the Scratchers.

After dinner, which Sebastien ended up staying for, their uncle told them it was time to come in for the night. Colin went in first, not wanting to watch Meghan and Sebastien awkwardly say goodnight to each other.

"Night, Sebastien," Colin called out, taking one last glance in Jae's direction.

"Yeah, later, Col."

Before Meghan could follow him inside, Sebastien pulled her into the shadow of the trailer, so they could not be seen.

"What?" she asked anxiously.

"I...I wanted to say, I'm sorry," he stuttered, keeping his gaze on his feet.

"Sorry for what?"

"Earlier today, we all sort of ganged up on you. I thought maybe we might have hurt your feelings, or something." He squirmed.

"Oh, that," was the only reply she could muster. Meghan thought back to her talk with Kanda. And although she was still afraid of things changing, she thought maybe it was time to talk to Sebastien, really talk to him.

"I was upset," she admitted. "So many strange things happening."

"That's why I started feeling bad, a lot *has* happened. I am sorry."

"Nothing makes sense to me anymore," she continued. "I hate that."

"I would bet that after tonight everything will go back to normal," he reassured her.

Meghan shifted her feet in the dirt and took a deep breath.

"I have this feeling, Sebastien. It keeps telling me nothing will be the same again."

He put his arm on her shoulder to comfort her and smiled his famous smile. For a moment, she lost all her worry and smiled back.

Meghan knew her uncle would be calling her inside any second.

"I better head in," she sighed.

"Yeah, tomorrow then."

He started to turn away and as he did, an uncontrollable urge surged through Meghan. Without thinking twice about it, she sprang at Sebastien, planting a kiss on his unsuspecting lips. She could not believe she had done it! Her heart skipped twenty beats.

Before Sebastien could respond, Meghan darted away. She saw, from the corner of her eye, that he stood frozen in place and to her incredible delight, he was beaming. She rushed inside drowning herself under her bed covers. Before she could stop it, Colin was in her thoughts.

"Oh, come off it! I don't want to hear about that!"

Meghan was too electrified to get angry.

"Then stay out!"

"Fine, goodnight." he said grumpily.

Their uncle came to the door.

"No talking, out loud or how ever else you do it. I want to hear snoring," he chuckled. He walked into their room and gave one of those speeches that grown ups give, and kids despise. Meghan thought she had heard enough of that for one day, but listened anyway, her heart still strumming.

"Look at you two, practically all grown up."

Meghan's first thought was that he had seen her kiss Sebastien, or worse, heard them talking.

"Before I know it," continued their uncle, "you'll be all grown up and living lives of your own."

"No need to worry," said Colin. "We will be around for a while yet. I mean, I can't legally leave until I'm sixteen."

His uncle laughed and ruffed up his hair. "Goodnight," he said, lingering at their door, before closing it. The twins did not speak after that, but also did not sleep. They continually checked the time for when Jae would be passing by them. The campground was in complete silence. No breeze rattled against the trailer, no peepers peeped in the night air and thankfully, there wo no cry of the Scratchers.

The twins felt that it was *too* quiet and wished that something would happen. It was ten o'clock now, another ninety minutes and he would be leaving for the fallen pine tree. Sleep came in waves after that. What felt like hours passed, when an echo pushed its way into the minds of the twins, rousting them from their fitful slumber.

"Scratchers!" gasped Colin, sitting up.

Meghan jumped softly out of her bunk and began dressing, and for the first time, Colin did not argue. Meghan opened the secret door and they slipped out.

"We are *so* grounded," Colin murmured as they crawled away.

"I am thinking a full year this time," agreed Meghan. A few minutes of running later, they were at the path's edge leading to the pine tree. Meghan noticed Colin's empty hands.

"Col, where's the book?"

He felt around as if the book would be up his sleeve.

"I can't believe it," he stammered.

"Forget it, there's no time, but be ready to do that spell." She started running down the path.

"I'm ready," he yelled. "I am just not sure it is going to work," he added under his breath.

It had to be nearly time for the door to open. The Scratchers howled, stopping the twins in their tracks. They saw a blast of light over the trees.

Jae was fighting!

They raced as fast as they dared, trying not to stumble over jutting tree roots and jagged rocks. Soon, the clearing was in front of them. Jae stood alone, close to one of the fallen pine tree's empty, but still dark rooms. He did not hear them come up behind him. The Scratchers' howls were deafening.

The twins watched as two began to dive from behind Jae, while he held the ones in front at bay. Jae nearly fell over when a voice shouted behind him.

"Emissio!"

Colin's magic still worked!

"What are you doing here?" Jae screamed in dismay over the noise of the flying beasts. "You'll be..."

Meghan did not allow him to finish.

"We remember what you said, Jae, but you cannot do this alone."

Fear rapidly turned to acceptance, as he knew she was right.

"How much longer?" asked Meghan, staying between the two boys.

"Any second now," Jae said, over the noise.

Colin helped Jae fend off the Scratchers, now constantly diving into the blasts. One of them was nearly breaking through when finally, a light began emanating from within the empty rooms of the fallen pine tree.

"Hurry, Jae, go through," said Meghan.

"We'll be fine," said Colin, ending his own spell.

"Where's your book?" Jae asked frantically.

"Ah, sorry, forgot it hurrying to get here."

"Jae, just go, you have to," insisted Meghan.

Two shapes emerged from the now lit pine tree. Jae let go of his spell appearing weak, and was caught by a man the twins assumed to be his father.

"I cannot believe you let yourself get stuck behind! Do you have any idea what this last month has been like for us?" the man shouted.

"How mean!" the twins thought in unison. "Shouldn't he be happy to see him?"

Jae's father then noticed the twins. His face contorted fiercely.

The second man that had come through shot spells at the Scratchers, pushing them higher into the sky.

"Dad, do you have to? If not for them, I don't think I would have made it."

His father's eyes darted between the twins and Jae.

"I am sorry son. Rules are rules." He pushed Jae into the pine room. He waved to the twins one last time, dissolving into the light.

His voice echoed back to them. "I'm sorry," he said, knowing they would soon lose all memory of him.

Jae's father approached the twins as the second man neared the doorway of the pine tree. The Scratchers were looming overhead reorganizing for another attack.

Out of nowhere, one lone flying beast flew over the twins, knocking them to the ground. Another dove head first into Jae's father, catching his shoulder and digging in deeply; so deep, that the sharp talon cracked and snapped off, remaining in Mr. Mochrie's shoulder.

The creature backed away in agonizing pain at the loss of its talon. Jae's father, also screaming in pain, rolled over on the ground, close to the still brightly lit pine room.

The second man still defended on the other side of the tree. The twins, now on the ground, crawled carefully over to Jae's father.

"I'm okay, he winced. "Stay close to the ground." Jae's father nudged the twins to move closer to the edge of the tree for extra cover.

"I assume that Jae has told you what I must do."

They nodded yes, not taking their fearful eyes off the Scratchers, now preparing to dive again.

"Before I do it, and even though you will forget, I must say thank you. I am truly sorry for what I must do."

Meghan and Colin knew they had done the right thing and no punishment, however great, could change their minds. With eyes closed, they waited for the spell to take away their memories of Jae. Wondering exactly what they would remember.

"You will have about five minutes until the spell takes effect," he informed them. "As soon as I say it, run as fast as you can. We will take care of the Scratchers."

A panic-stricken voice rang out from behind Jae's father.

"Irving, in front of you!"

No more than he'd said it, the twins saw the Scratchers diving directly for them. Jae's father attempted to stand and speak at the same time but the spell missed completely. The creature hit Irving Mochrie with a crushing blow, dragging him across the ground with its curved claw. He fell to the ground with a new gash across his chest, a few feet away from the entrance to his freedom. The man helping Jae's father worked his way toward Irving, still sending defensive spells, which were growing weaker.

Echoes of voices began to escape from inside the shining room. They had not seen what had happened. They were yelling for the two to hurry. The man helping Irving was now over him, and ignoring the twins.

He dragged Irving Mochrie's body closer to the pine room; he was unconscious and bleeding profusely. Colin and Meghan tried to keep low and help the man. Irving was not a large man but his weight was heavy.

"He looks bad," sent Colin uneasily.

"I hope he isn't…" Meghan could not muster out the word. The man let go of Irving, leaving the twins to try to pull him closer.

"Get him close as you can, I will keep defending. Then run, and once I see you're away, I will take him through," he said. "You are very brave and the Svoda will have to trust you with our secret."

There was no time for a reply. The man fought hard, shouting his spell repeatedly, as the twins struggled to move Irving closer to the doorway. The light inside was growing fainter, and blood was pouring from his chest, leaving a trail behind his dragging body.

As they got Irving as close as possible to the pine room, without going in themselves, a blood-curdling scream broke their concentration. The other man flew through the air and into one of the other doorways. He disappeared into the light.

"That's not good," Colin said blankly.

The Scratchers reformed overhead.

"Now what?" yelled Meghan. "I don't think we can push him in!"

Voices were still echoing, but becoming more distant.

"Maybe we can drag him in before the light goes out. We cannot allow him to get stuck here," said Colin, pulling once again. Without arguing, both twins worked together and pulled Jae's father into the room. Once in, they could feel the pull coming from the other side.

Shadows of people from the other side danced around the pine room as the pull sucked Irving's body through. The twins let go of him, holding on to the tree, trying not to get sucked through too.

"We have to get out of here," struggled Colin.

Meghan and Colin pulled hard and kicked their legs to the ground, bouncing out of the pine tree.

Then, they froze in complete horror!

Uncle Arnon!

Surrounded by the Scratchers!

"No!" screamed Meghan.

The light was nearly gone behind them. There would be no more help from the Svoda on the other side.

Colin decided to break the rules and no longer cared who knew about his magic, if it even still worked now that Jae was gone.

"Emissio!" he boomed.

An angry blast tore at the howling creatures. Arnon took a few steps forward and to the twins' bewilderment, he appeared not worried, scared, or surprised, but instead beamed with pride.

"He's going to be killed," thought Meghan, seeing the Scratchers already reorganizing.

"Why did he follow us?" questioned Colin.

Above, two of the regrouped Scratchers dove directly for Meghan and Colin. Arnon saw this and took off, darting athletically through the remaining creatures, as they plunged toward him, their wings poised for the kill.

When Arnon was ten feet away from the twins, he heaved himself into the air, spinning toward them. A Scratcher hovered over Arnon's whirling frame, its wings ready to enclose around him. It shrieked hideously over its impending victory.

Arnon threw something at Colin.

It hit him with such force that he fell back, disappearing into the pine room.

Without a second thought, Meghan dove after him, hoping to catch Colin before he went all the way through.

Then, the fallen pine tree went dark.

##

Thank you for reading the Fated Saga.

If you enjoyed this book, please leave a review. Reviews help authors *a ton,* when it comes to rankings and such on Amazon.

To read more books in this series please visit: **www.racheldaigle.com**

While there, be sure to sign up for New Book Release Alerts & News Updates. Not only will you be the first to know about exciting news and book releases, but you'll get FREE side stories, cut scenes and previews from each series.

Fated Saga Book List:

Book One: Awaken
Book Two: Shifting
Book Three: Embrace
Book Four: Broken
Book Five: Divided
Book Six: Taken
Book Seven: Control
Book Eight: TBA (expected Summer 2014)
Book Nine: TBA (expected Summer 2014)

Made in the USA
Lexington, KY
09 December 2014